Suddenly
MRS. DARCY

JENETTA JAMES

Meryton Press

Oysterville, WA

SUDDENLY MRS DARCY

ISBN: 978-1-936009-42-8

Graphic design by Ellen Pickels

Prologue

I have never felt less sure of myself than I feel now. The candlelight flickers over the plain walls and shadowy furnishings of this room. Darkness and damp press against the small windows. An empty rambling countryside lies beyond, and the rumble of unknown revellers roars quietly below. I know he will come to me, and I pull the heavy blanket higher against my person. I can hardly credit I am here, nor know how the compromise of my life shall ever be made right.

When he does come, I know I must welcome him. It cannot be that he truly wants me, for we are strangers, and in his manner, he has made it plain. He says little, and in view of what has happened, I dread to imagine what he thinks. Even my mother, a woman of mean understanding, little information, and uncertain temper, seems to know all is not quite as it should be. She knows, as I do and as he does, that she is the author of our situation. I mull, not for the first time, the way in which this began. The confusion and speed of events and the ambiguous nature of the tricks played upon me scream through my mind. I can make no sense of his part. Is he motivated by honour or hatred of scandal or pity, or some other unknown creature in his head? Does he lack the imagination to act other than he has done? I have only the scantest knowledge of him. You could not call it intimacy; you could not call it friendship. Even so, it is a secret between us that he is in some sense guilty if not exactly guilty as charged. However, we are here in this place, and the best must be made of it if we are not to run mad.

Occasionally, I hear a tread upon the stair and I start, marshalling my courage and straightening my face. But then the tread moves in another direction or returns to the public bar. Some servant perhaps or another guest—not him, coming for me. I turn onto my side in the unfamiliar bed, thinking that, by moving my limbs, I may still their trembling. Apart from the fear of what must come, I am also tired to the bone.

The journey north began almost immediately after our wedding and is not yet complete; it has been long and the weather treacherous. Mr Darcy sat opposite me in the carriage and said little. In my head, he is "Mr Darcy." Our connection, short and strange, does not seem to merit any other appellation. In the darkness, I miss my sister Jane and the sweet smells and familiar shapes of our chamber at Longbourn where I have slept all my life. The memory of my mother's advice, given in that chamber on the subject of this night, returns to me. I begin to wish it would start rather than hound me by being so protracted in the anticipation.

And so it does start. Steps on the stair do not recede or return. Instead, they grow louder, heavier, and closer; they pause only briefly before I hear a tap upon the door. "Come," I say, not knowing whether it would be better to say nothing for he knows I am in here. Where else should I be but in this room in this bed? I have nowhere to run as he well knows.

His appearance in the light of the doorway makes me feel small, but I resist the urge to shrink further to the edge of the bed. Something inside me rises, and though I am fearful, I raise my head slightly and look at his face. It wears a blank expression, and as he closes the door behind him, he asks if I am comfortable.

"Yes, sir. Thank you. I am."

He sits upon the bed and stretches out his hand to me, not touching. "Good. I hope that you are. Madam. Elizabeth. I know you must be fatigued." He seems to want to say more but does not. The emptiness of the air and the words unspoken swell the space between us, and I remember my resolve.

"I am not so fatigued, sir." I try to smile and not appear embarrassed by my circumstances. A shadow of a reply plays across his lips in acknowledgement, and he begins to undress. I turn my head, for watching a man disrobe is wholly without my experience, and I had not anticipated it. I knew it was not a spectacle I should usually witness since Mr Darcy would normally be undressed by his valet. But this night we have been, as so often during our short association, wrong-footed by matters outside our control. Only one chamber was available, so only one chamber do we have.

And only one bed—so I know I must make the best of it. When he wears only his lawn shirt, he lifts the side of the blanket and, looking at my face for only a moment, gets in. He also looks at the candlelight flickering across the empty wall before turning to me and saying "Elizabeth, come," as he takes my shoulder and rolls me towards his embrace. My mother had told me it would be over quickly, and so indeed it was. He is not rough and has the goodness to warn me it may hurt at first. It does hurt, but I do not cry out; I will not allow myself to do so. I simply lie before him and allow him to part my legs and enter me as I had been told he would. I find I am not prepared for the odd feeling of his great weight upon me nor the solitary feelings of indistinct woe that beset me as I lie on my side afterwards, feeling his wetness, hearing his breathing, and hopeless of sleep for myself.

Chapter One

The excitement rendered to our household by the arrival in the neighbourhood of Mr Bingley and his party had been great. I have wondered since whether over-excitement caused by his leasing the nearby manor at Netherfield Park was at the root of what then took place. Whatever the truth, the introduction of a rich and single gentleman, ready to smile and dance, had quite kicked up the dust of our lives. Excitement would have ensued whether or not he had a preference for my sister Jane. But as it was, he had taken immediate notice of her beauty and goodness, and our mother was in raptures. The rest of Mr Bingley's party had been the fly in the ointment from the start. His sisters, Miss Bingley and Mrs Hurst, were ladies of fashion, more pleased with themselves than what they saw. His friend Mr Darcy was as haughty as he was disagreeable. It was said he was very rich, but this seemed to one and all to be small consolation for a sour disposition. They looked at us and our little community and found us wanting. I found each of the sisters and Mr Darcy studying me on occasion but did not particularly wonder at their reasons. I was too thrilled for Jane, and I was invigorated, as we all were, by the prospect of *things happening*.

When Jane took ill at Netherfield Hall, I had an opportunity to see more of our new neighbours. The news reached our family that Jane was abed with a fever after she had taken supper with Mr Bingley's sisters, so I walked across the fields to her aid. I am a strong walker and think nothing of three miles on a familiar path when my sister is poorly at the other end. I detected some reticence at my appearance from the ladies of the household and Mr Darcy, but I did not think on it. During my stay, I had a number of uncomfortable exchanges with Mr Darcy and often found him glancing in my direction. He and I communicated only by way of disagreement, and I began to feel that our being together in the same room was a punishment for everyone else present. Any discussion between us seemed to descend inexorably into an argument. We were discordant notes trapped briefly in the same tune. We were not friends, and I did not seek his approval any more than he sought mine. Apart from this reflection, I did not think about him at all. Blessedly, Jane was recovered in three days, and we were home.

No sooner did Mr Bingley and his household establish themselves at Netherfield than the regiment arrived among us and quartered themselves at Meryton. Suddenly, our village was crawling with redcoats, and all of us, particularly my younger sisters Kitty and Lydia, were in raptures. In this way, Mr Wickham came to be among us. He was, I thought privately, the handsomest officer of the regiment and very agreeable. His easy manners put all at leisure with him, and his conversation flowed naturally. I was quite taken with him and flattered he always sought me out. In one of our earliest conversations, he had told me of his connection to Mr Darcy and their growing up together on Mr Darcy's family estate in Derbyshire: Mr Darcy as son and heir, and Mr. Wickham as the son of old Mr Darcy's steward. Mr Wickham had played as a child with Mr Darcy, but in adulthood, Mr Darcy had done him a great wrong. Mr Darcy's father was godfather to Mr Wickham and favoured him greatly. The old man funded his godson's education and planned for him to enter the church. However, when old Mr Darcy died, his son refused to honour his father's request that Mr Wickham have a living within his gift. Such injustice had forced Mr Wickham into the military life, but he was as sanguine as he was charming and seemed to rise above the spite of Mr Darcy. I admired him greatly and could not be in his company enough.

To this ferment was added the visit to Longbourn of our cousin Mr Collins. Older than his years and lengthy in his conversation, Mr Collins is a clergyman who shall inherit Longbourn on our father's death. I have never troubled myself with the origins or mechanics of *the entail*. It is simply a fact of our lives that, when our father dies, our home shall become the property of a distantly related stranger. His arrival at Longbourn was to disabuse us all of any mystery or romance that may previously have attached to him. He had not been with us for ten minutes before we were all assured he talked far too much and thought far too little. He flattered where flattery was neither necessary nor welcome. In relation to his parish patroness, Lady Catherine de Bourgh, we were left in no doubt of her wealth, prestige, and condescension towards him. He had spoken in his letter to my father of looking to make amends to us for the injury he would ultimately do us by inheriting our home. I was, therefore, alarmed and disquieted to find him on a number of occasions looking in my direction, tilting his greasy head, and creasing his face in a smile.

Happy was the day that all the families in the neighbourhood received their invitation to a ball at Netherfield. Dances were requested and dresses considered, and we were all aflutter. On the morning of the ball, Mama accosted me as I returned to Longbourn after my morning walk. It was immediately apparent she had something to say that she meant me to heed but suspected I would not. "Elizabeth, come here." She beckoned me conspiratorially although there was nobody else there to see. The air was chill, and the trees had lost their leaves. We walked together in the bare, bracken-littered garden. "Now Lizzy, you will be *very attentive* to Mr Collins this evening, for he is particular for your company, and you would do well not to put him off."

"I have agreed to dance the first two dances with him, Mama. You know I cannot escape."

"And why ever should you wish to escape, child? What a notion! You should be very particular to please Mr Collins as he has shown a preference for you. I hope he will ask you to dance the supper dance with him as well, for then you would secure him throughout the meal. Yes, that would be a great advantage. I shall find some way of suggesting it to him."

"Mama, I beg you would not suggest anything more to him. I shall dance with him—of course, I shall—but two dances will be quite enough. I do not wish to spend the whole evening with him. And as for supper—surely, we all endure enough of his conversation at home!"

I recognized the ire rising in her and the mistaken belief that I misunderstood her meaning. "Lizzy, you do not know of what you speak. This is not merely a matter of supper and dancing. I have very good reason to believe it is more serious. Mr Collins has resolved to choose a bride from among our daughters, and he favours you, Lizzy. He will make you an offer —I am sure of it—and soon. You must be ready. You must not put him off."

"Mama, please." I could not let her go on. "Our cousin, he is ... well, he is simply not a man whom I could ever imagine marrying. And I am very pleased to say that he has not asked me."

"Pleased! Pleased!" she barked. "Pleased to be the ruin of your family when you could secure the future of your mother and your poor sisters; you say you will not. How can you think so? I am ashamed of you! I suppose you think there is some alternative! Who do you think will come for you? Do you expect a second Mr Bingley to come into the neighbourhood, or maybe you fancy a life as Mrs Wickham, eh? Well, you are a foolish girl. It will never come to be. You will never get a better offer than Mr Collins, and then when your father dies, we shall not be turned out of our home. You cannot refuse him."

"I can refuse him, Mama, and I will." I tried, not completely successfully, to keep my voice level whilst Mama's climbed in volume and octave.

"You selfish creature. *You selfish creature.* How have I raised such a selfish girl? I do not know! Your father shall hear of this. You may not pick and choose, Elizabeth; you owe this to your family. I expect you to attend to Mr Collins this evening and attend him well." The lace framing her face shook as she spoke, and she looked away from me in fury.

"You ask too much, Mama. I will not do it. My feelings forbid it in every respect."

At that moment, my sister Mary appeared to say that Mama was wanted in the house. I do not suspect her of having listened to our exchange; my sisters and I were so used to Mama's histrionics that they did not signify. However, I knew I had rattled my mother, and she was working her anger around and around in her mind. I saw her glance at my every move and tighten her lips, ruminating on the best manner to foist Mr Collins upon me.

It did not do to spoil such a merry day in pondering this discussion with Mama, so I did not do so. The house was alive with laughter and the hubbub of ribbon swapping and gown altering as my sisters and I prepared for the ball. Our poor father retreated to his library as our mother pronounced loudly and repeatedly who should look well in what. My sisters bickered over pieces of lace and ornamented one another's hair with beads and flowers. It was dusk when our family carriage drew up outside Netherfield, and I felt the wonder of seeing that familiar house losing the daylight, bedecked with lanterns, humming with all the people of our acquaintance, and more.

My dances with Mr Collins were not over as soon as I would have liked; he stumbled and babbled his way through them in a most conspicuous manner. I would never have danced with Mr Darcy had I been able to find a reason to refuse him. But upon the heels of my set with Mr Collins, I could not. There was nothing I expected less, so when he asked me, I was at a loss to say anything other than, "Thank you."

The set was a trial for us both. When I could withstand his silence no longer, I tried to tempt him into conversation and got almost nowhere. When we did talk, we descended quickly into argument. He had seen me in conversation with Mr Wickham days before, and he made some remark that Mr Wickham can make friends but not retain them. I could not bear to leave his arrogance unchecked.

"He has been so unhappy as to lose your friendship in a way he is likely to suffer from all his life," I said, not looking into his eyes, for our dance did not allow it. I felt him stiffen beside me, and I was not sorry I had made him uncomfortable. Why should he not feel discomforted in public when Mr. Wickham had suffered so grievously?

"You take a great interest in that gentleman's affairs, Miss Bennet. Have you been long acquainted?"

"A man's character may be plain upon first meeting. I always believe in first impressions, and a long acquaintance is by no means essential to trust a man's word."

As the dance drew to its end, he bowed to my curtsey and said, almost in a whisper, "I would beg you, Miss Bennet, that you not trust that particular man's word. It is not worthy of you." Unconvinced as I was, I was also intrigued, and when he held his arm out to me, I placed my hand upon it and walked with him.

"You cannot expect praise, Mr Darcy, for such stern words in a ballroom. A dance is for making mirth, is it not? It is not for slandering an agreeable gentleman whom you have injured."

I felt him tense and knew at once I had gone too far. Unseen by others, I felt his arm pull me towards the edge of the room and through the open door of a dimly lit salon. As we entered, the daughters of Mrs Long, whom I have known all my life, left laughing and nudging one another, anticipating their dances. My sister Mary, brushing at a mark upon her skirts and frowning, was behind them. Mr Darcy dropped his arm and turned his back to me, running his fingers through his hair. Feeling his disturbance—and my own at being alone with him—I turned to leave, but he stopped me.

"Miss Bennet, I hope I have never done anything to lead you to distrust me."

"Certainly not, Mr Darcy. I am sure you agree I hardly know you."

"But to know and not to know are relative terms." He lingered, seeming to form sentences in his mind, only to discard them and say nothing. I had almost exhausted my intrigue and resolved to depart the room when his eyes held mine, and he placed his hand on my shoulder, lowering his head to speak quietly. Shocked as I was by his touch, he only meant to speak, of that I am sure.

But the moment was broken by a shriek from behind me. I spun around and, seeing my mother, knew before she spoke the litany of possibilities playing about her mind. I could see in her expression and the manner in which she did not meet my eyes that the plot was hatching in her thoughts almost quicker than she could give it voice. I also knew that, once she had started, she would not be able to stop. "Elizabeth! Mr Darcy! You are kissing my daughter. What are you about? Whatever can you mean by this? Mary, find your father. Find Mr Bennet!"

Mrs Long was close behind and, needing only seconds of preparation, was in hysterics as well. The salon, so quiet and peaceful a moment before, seemed suddenly to burst with unwanted and confusing sounds, women jostling, questions, and expressions of astonishment. For a moment, the horror of it struck me dumb. I forced myself to speak.

"*Mama*, please, you are mistaken. Mr Darcy was not kissing me or doing anything untoward. We were *talking*." I tried to speak to her quietly and directly, ignoring Mrs Long and the others who had appeared.

"I saw him. I saw you. Do not contradict me, you foolish girl. Why would you protect him? You are mistaken if you think I will stand and watch while my daughter is taken advantage of. Certainly not! And you sell yourself cheap if you allow him liberties, Elizabeth. Where is Mr Bennet? Fetch Mr Bennet at once!"

"Mama, please, there is no need for this. The light in here is poor. You have made a mistake."

I felt then the pressure of his hand on the small of my back and was silent. "I will speak with your father." He did not look at me as he said this, and I did not look at him as he left the salon. Neither did I follow him, but I saw as he approached Papa and led him out of the ballroom. Mortification consumed me, and even Mama's shrieking commentary was lost to my hearing. I longed for my sister Jane, but she was engaged, dancing with Mr Bingley.

The time seemed to drain away, and I was in anguish at what was now passing between my father and Mr Darcy. At length, my father appeared and seemed almost to be reading from a script as he spoke. "Mrs Bennet, Elizabeth, there are to be no more scenes this evening. We shall not offend or surprise any of our neighbours if we leave this place in half an hour, and that is what we shall do. There is to be no discussion, and we shall leave quietly. I shall ask Jane to thank Miss Bingley, and apart from that, I would like you all to keep yourselves close. Quite enough has been broadcast as it is. I have asked Sir William to look after Mr Collins for the remainder of the ball, and he shall convey him to Longbourn when the Lucas family returns home to Lucas Lodge. I regret the need to impose myself on our neighbours in this way, but there it is."

My mother knew better than to contradict him in these rare moments of assertiveness. My mind was wracked with shame to think what Mr Darcy must have said. That gentleman I did not see and believed he must have left for his chambers or quit the country altogether in horror at my family's behaviour. Although I disliked him, I could not help but be troubled by his having such proof of our unworthiness. For him to appear as we approached our carriage to leave was the last thing I expected, but appear he did. He nodded to Papa, handed me into the carriage first of all our family, and said in a whisper, "I shall call upon you in the morning."

There was nothing more, and I was mystified. The carriage ride home to Longbourn was a dreadful affair, and even my sister Lydia was too afraid of Papa's expression to speak. As we neared home, Papa spoke again, hardly looking at us. "Mary, Kitty, Lydia, when we reach Longbourn, you may retire immediately, please. Mrs Bennet, I believe you and I must speak alone in my library. Lizzy, you will wait in the drawing room with Jane until I am ready to speak with you."

And so that was how it was. My younger sisters, almost teary with the abrupt end of their evening, were sent early to bed in confusion while Jane and I sat waiting, knowing little more of what was afoot. Eventually, Mama appeared and called us to Papa's library. "Lizzy, Jane, come in and sit down. Well, Lizzy, I had not expected to part with you under these circumstances, and I am not proud to do so, but I am sure you see the necessity of it. You are fortunate that your young man appears to be reasonably honourable if not reasonably cautious in his behaviour."

Horror at the implications of his words overtook me, and I glanced around the room in panic, noting that Mama looked away. My temperature rose, and the books that lined the room seemed to leap from their shelves and dance before my eyes. "Papa, please stop. There has been an awful mistake. Mr Darcy is *not* my young man. He never has been."

"Elizabeth, if you are observed kissing a man in a public place, then I am afraid he *is* your young man, whatever you may protest."

"There was no kiss, Papa. None at all. Mr Darcy was talking to me. Mama, please, you must realise you were mistaken. That is how it looked to you, but it is not how it was. This is all so wrong. It is so mistaken."

"Lizzy, that is enough. Your mother observed you clearly, as I understand did Mrs Long and her daughters. It was plain enough, and you must realise all the families of our acquaintance will now know of this affair. Your Mr Darcy is willing to marry you, and in the circumstances, there is nothing else to be done."

My mind reeled with the words, and although I saw my sister Jane take my hand, I hardly felt it. After further conversation, which I cannot now recall, she helped me up the stairs to the bed we shared. The rest of the night was darkness.

Chapter Two

I would have sought out my mother in the morning, but I knew it would serve no purpose. A kind of fatalistic acceptance stole over me, and I awaited Mr Darcy's call in silence. How the news of my situation spread around Longbourn, I know not, but at breakfast, everyone seemed to be aware of it. My sister Lydia, never quiet for long, celebrated her share of the advantage. "Well, now that you are to be married, Lizzy, you shall not keep Wickham to yourself any longer. It is just as well, as Kitty and I would like time with him. And you shall get into trouble if you leave Mr Darcy's side!" she quipped, and she and Kitty dissolved into laughter. There was much more, but for the most part, I did not listen.

When Mr Darcy did arrive, he tethered his horse and made straight for Papa's library. He did not come to the drawing room where my mother, sisters, and I sat around like birds on a lawn, and however ashamed I felt, I was also affronted by his rudeness to us. Eventually, I was called to the library. "Lizzy, come in. Mr Darcy has asked to speak with you in private, and I have agreed. I am leaving the door open and do not expect it to be closed in my absence." I gasped slightly, still unused to Papa's new manner of addressing me, but he simply left without further ado, and I was forced to face my visitor. Mr Darcy paced the small room for a short time before turning to me and taking my hand purposely.

"Miss Bennet, I hope you have slept well."

"No, I have not, sir. I am sure that you have not. What do you mean by taking responsibility for this situation? I hope you do not believe I would ever have insisted on anything."

He cut me off abruptly, squeezing my hand. "Miss Bennet, please do not distress yourself. The circumstances are what they are, and I have spoken with your father. I do not wish to speak of it further. I cannot rejoice in how this has come about, but I am an honourable man, and you should know I would not abandon you."

"But Mr Darcy you have been—you *know* you are—the victim of a mistake as to the facts. I am sure in time that this could be forgot and we would all be as we were. I—"

"It would be as well to say no more about it. It is not as I would have wished, but there is nothing to be done. I do not wish for you to feel uneasy and I...I...you need have no fear of your future. Having said that, I do not wish to linger. The circumstances of our...*engagement*"—he seemed to chew over the word as though it were gristle in his meat—"are such that I wish to be married quickly and leave this place. I have discussed this with your father, and we have agreed I shall ride to London today to obtain a special licence in order that we may be married next week."

"Next week!" I repeated with more feeling than civility.

"Yes, next week. You understand, I am sure."

In horror, I did understand. I understood there was no escape from a union with this high-handed and disagreeable man, and the only advantage, though he loved me not, was that he appeared to wish me no ill. He assured me he would return as soon as may be, even that same day if the weather allowed. In my mind, I laughed at this suggestion, for I could bear his absence well enough. As it was, he kissed my hand, mounted his horse, and was gone.

Time being short, it was resolved I should be wed in Jane's best gown, which was the finest in the house. The next afternoon, I stood on a box in our chamber as Hill pinned the hem when Jane entered clutching a letter and looking about her. The letter was from Miss Bingley, and its message was that the whole party had quit Hertfordshire for town for a stay of indefinite length. Netherfield was shut up, and we knew not when it would be opened again. I could not help but think the circumstances of my engagement had somehow caused this. Jane, who had done no wrong, perched on the edge of our bed like a sparrow, and I felt wretched for her. Although we felt downcast, there was no time for self-pity since Kitty and Lydia roared up the stairs and into our chamber, crying out their news.

"Lizzy! Lizzy! Mr Darcy is come; he is come... Or at least he is coming!"

"Save your breath to cool your porridge, Kitty, I shall tell Lizzy! We have seen him. We have seen him, and we ran from Meryton to Longbourn to be assured of beating him. He rode his great horse into the village and looked very tired. He entered the inn! We watched him go in, and then we ran home. I bet you are glad we warned you that he was coming."

"For it would not do for him to find you in your shift!" added Kitty as they both collapsed laughing.

He did not find me in my shift. By the time he arrived on his horse and looking grave, my sisters, my mother, and I were all sensibly dressed and sitting in the parlour. His short absence had given my spirits time to calm. I thought of Jane, my sisters, and the benefit my marriage might be to them if I could only make it so. But I was not yet used to the idea of him, and as he was announced and stalked into the room, my heart raced. He nodded acknowledgements to my family and said almost nothing. When I could bear the silence and awkwardness no longer, I suggested a walk to which he readily consented. Mary and Mr Collins accompanied us as chaperones, and gathering my bonnet, gloves, and spencer, I could hardly remove quickly enough from the house.

I knew Mr Darcy was equally desirous of fresh air and escape, yet he said little until we had substantially outpaced my sister and cousin. "Miss Bennet, I am sorry to have been gone so long. I had hoped to obtain the licence and return within a day, but in the end I was forced to spend the night in town. I had no intention of leaving you alone for so long before our wedding."

"Our wedding. You speak so easily of it, but I hardly know anything of the event. Maybe you can tell me, sir, what you seem to have already decided."

Apparently not taking the meaning of my barb, he took my hand and squeezed it. "Yes, of course. I have the licence, and I thought Wednesday would be appropriate. I have spoken to the rector in Meryton, and it can be done. The ceremony will be simple, and we will depart from the church. The journey to Pemberley is at least two days, perhaps more."

"When am I to bid goodbye to my family and acquaintances, sir?"

"I propose you do that before the service, Elizabeth. You know I do not wish to delay our departure."

"What of your family, sir? You have told me nothing of them or who shall be there."

"I have asked a cousin, Colonel Fitzwilliam, to stand up with me. Your introduction to the others will come later."

"A cousin? Nobody else? Not even your sister?" I had heard much of the superlative Miss Darcy, most of it from the lips of Miss Bingley. Mr Darcy's sister, I had been told, was accomplishment itself, playing the pianoforte with excellence and acquitting herself without a hint of error. Mr Wickham had accused the young lady of pride, and in view of Miss Bingley's approval and Mr Darcy's tendencies, I could well believe it.

"No. Georgiana cannot possibly come here. You will meet her soon enough, and I hope you will be happy with each other, but I would not bring her here."

I felt the flames of anger rise inside me and lick my face and hands. I could hardly control the fury within me and looked at our feet pacing the frozen ground. Finding my courage, I continued. "Are we not to expect Mr Bingley and his sisters?"

"No. They are in town, and they do not expect to return for the wedding. I hope we will see them when we are in town, but they will not be here next week."

"I am shocked by that, sir. What can have called Mr Bingley away so urgently?"

He hesitated, his grip on my hand slackening. "I do not know. Some matter of business that could not be delayed."

"I wonder, then, that his sisters travelled with him!"

"Miss Bingley and Mrs Hurst both prefer town."

"As they have made abundantly clear." I saw a slight smile trace across his lips at this, and he stopped, taking my hand firmly again.

"Elizabeth...I feel...I hope we have not made a bad start in knowing one another." He had said my name for the first time, and I looked away, discomforted. "I did not mean to desert you so soon, and I do mean for you to know all of my family. But not here at Longbourn. My sister is young and gentle and not used to raucous company. Especially with the regiment here...well, it would be insupportable. I wish to take you home. I hope you comprehend that."

"I believe I do," I said in spite of myself. For all of my resentments against him and the anger in my heart, I felt a warmth stirring within me for which I could not account.

"Do you stay at Netherfield, sir?"

"No, I am staying at the inn in Meryton."

"I hope you are comfortable there. It can hardly be what you are accustomed to."

"I am not such a princeling, Elizabeth. It is perfectly adequate, and it is not for long."

In the days that followed, we undertook a number of such walks with Mary and Mr Collins dawdling behind us. I will not say *enjoyed* because that would not be quite right. Mr Darcy took prodigious care of my comfort, handing me over stiles I could easily manage myself and guiding me around tree roots that never would have tripped me. At times, he was warm and almost caring. At other times, he was wounding in his arrogance and disdain for my position in life. It was made plain to me, for example, that none of my clothes were adequate for his wife, and upon reaching Pemberley, I would need to acquire a whole new wardrobe. It seemed to me he considered it to be my fault that there was no time for me to do this before I was married. In that moment, I felt wretched that he looked upon me and disapproved of what he saw. At other times, he fuelled my ire, and I wanted nothing more than to defy and infuriate him.

Two days before our wedding, he observed me exchanging pleasantries with Mr. Wickham whilst out visiting with my sisters in Meryton. At the sight of Mr Darcy earnestly striding towards us, Mr Wickham bowed gracefully and departed, leaving me to face my betrothed.

"Elizabeth, I must ask you do not bargain words with that man. I have said before that Mr Wickham is not worthy of your good opinion, and I meant it."

I flushed with the embarrassment of being chastised in the street and despised myself for being so in his power. It occurred to me how I might have responded to him were we not engaged to be married, and I could not but lament my lack of freedom to speak as I wished.

"If you must direct me so, Mr Darcy—and I accept that it is your right to do so—will you not give me an explanation for your dictates?"

"What explanation could you need, Elizabeth? If you trust my judgement, then you are in need of no explanation."

"Well, if you trust my judgement, then why not confide in me? Mr Wickham appears to all the world as a respectable and pleasant gentleman. You do not like each other. That is clear. Since we are to be married, when you tell me not to speak to him, you know I must obey you. But you must allow me to be exceedingly perplexed by your attitude towards him. Or maybe you think it is not for me to ask questions or think on my own account?"

He took a sharp breath and slowed his pace, looking down at the frozen ground. "I do not—That is not what I think." Not looking at me, he continued. "I will tell you about Wickham, but would you allow it to wait? I do not wish to pass my engagement discussing him, and there will be time enough later. If you trust me now, I will explain later. Are we agreed?"

I pondered him and, not for the first time, was bewildered. He seemed to keep so much within himself and take pride in doing so. Nothing was said that had not been assessed and reassessed. No unaccounted for word seemed ever to pass his lips, and all about him was economized and deliberate. For myself, I was a talker. The tonic of good company and the unexpected turns in a long conversation with a willing partner—those were the things for me. I wondered how we should ever make a partnership: the strange, silent, controlled man and I.

Colonel Fitzwilliam arrived only the day before our wedding day. Anxious though I had been to meet Mr Darcy's cousin, it was immediately apparent that he was easy and charming where my betrothed was difficult and taciturn. Conversation became a great deal easier, and Colonel Fitzwilliam accompanied us on our final chaperoned walk before marriage. He spoke of things that Mr Darcy had never mentioned: of Miss Georgiana's shyness, trusted servants, and family traditions. He informed me that Lady Catherine de Bourgh, of whom my cousin Mr Collins spoke so oft, was Mr Darcy's aunt.

"Colonel Fitzwilliam, you shall have to continue with these lessons in order that I am quite prepared to face the Darcy family. Otherwise, I fear I shall be quite undone by such a daunting task!"

"My dear, Miss Bennet. Darcy should be arming you with all the gossip you need to face them! Although, of course, I am bound to say they are not that bad, and I hope they hold no fear for you. Our aunt Lady Catherine —well—she is an acquired taste to be sure, but my parents and my brother —they are not so terrifying, would you not agree, Darcy?"

"I wonder that anyone could terrify Miss Bennet, Fitzwilliam, but certainly not your parents."

"In any case, you will be bound to meet them very soon, for Matlock is only thirty miles from Pemberley."

"Does your family live in Matlock, sir?"

He smiled and seemed to stifle a laugh. "My parents are the Earl and Countess of Matlock, Miss Bennet," he said, looking more at Mr Darcy than at me. I seemed to ignite from the shame that my betrothed had not told me this himself.

And so it was that my marriage was a strange, hurried, and patched together affair that nobody seemed to enjoy. Although they knew it to be advantageous, my family struggled to cope with Mr Darcy's stern nature and willed the event to be over. I felt little different myself. The matter concluded, I kissed my parents and my sisters and boarded Mr Darcy's carriage, knowing not when I should return.

Chapter Three

When the carriage arrived, evening was settling in, and Pemberley was blanketed in snow. We had spent one further night on the road and had travelled hard all day to arrive before nightfall. He had woken me on our approach that I might view the house. I feared I had mistakenly fallen asleep against his chest since, after our first night at the inn, he had sat alongside me in the carriage. Thus, we had travelled for many miles, the wool of our sleeves brushing, our bodies close, and my mind disturbed by his proximity.

To say Pemberley is beautiful hardly credits it with the praise it deserves. It is a place for which neither God nor man could have done more, and I had never seen its equal. It is also vast. Its halls and walls spin out in all directions, covering huge swathes of ground and reaching great heights. When Mr Darcy handed me out of the carriage and I beheld the house from its threshold, I fancied it so large that I should be overwhelmed for the rest of my life. My neck would not crane far enough to see the roof, and my feet were too small for the mountain of steps before me. In a daze and on my husband's rigid arm, I was marched through the main rooms of the house. Oak panels and oil paintings seemed to close in upon me as I moved. A phalanx of faces, all bowing, curtseying, and making way for us, surrounded me. As we moved through them, I fought to regain my composure. It was not in my nature to be intimidated, and I was quite determined I would not be on this occasion.

Mr Darcy showed me to my chambers, which adjoined his. The bedchamber was quite four times the size of that which Jane and I shared at

Longbourn, and the bed so large, I fancied it looked like a ship.

"You will of course make any changes you deem appropriate."

"I am sure that will not be necessary, sir. The rooms are very elegant, and I am hardly a lady of fashion." I had not intended to sound sour but, knowing I had, decided not to regret it.

"Well, you may please yourself, Elizabeth. You may change what you wish to change and leave what you do not. You are the mistress of the house now, and it is your choice. I have only one request; I think we are rather beyond 'sir' now, do you not?" He raised his eyebrows. "Would you be willing to call me by my given name?"

"Yes, of course," I said, still shy of actually speaking it.

"Thank you." He gave me a look so strange and fixed that I felt compelled to turn away.

"Will you be ready to dine in an hour? I will see you in the small dining room."

With that, he left me to my muddled thoughts. Before too long a young woman appeared and introduced herself to me as Hannah, my lady's maid. She was small and neat, and her green eyes were framed by a barely concealed fringe of ginger curls. I immediately knew that we should be friends, and I allowed her to dress my hair slightly more extravagantly than was my wont and select a splendid but unknown blue gown from the wardrobe.

"Hannah, this gown is lovely, but it is not mine."

"It belongs to Miss Georgiana, madam. The master sent an express that a number of Miss Georgiana's gowns were to be given to you until you have obtained new. I had to guess at how much to take it up, but I see that it is about right. This colour favours you greatly, madam."

I studied the fine fabric and beautiful stitch work. It was a lovely gown, lovelier than any I had ever owned. It also looked as though it would fit me, and I wondered whether Miss Darcy and I were alike in size.

"Thank you. You have done an excellent job, but I am rather embarrassed. It would never do to meet Miss Darcy wearing her clothes!"

"I am sure that will not happen, madam. Miss Georgiana is staying with Lord and Lady Matlock and will not return yet awhile. The master has said I am to accompany you into Lambton to obtain new this week, so there is no need to fret. In any case, Miss Georgiana is a lovely person, and I am sure you have nothing to fear in her."

More opinions on the famous Miss Darcy! I recalled again Mr. Wickham's description of her as "excessively proud" and wondered what the truth of the matter may be. It occurred to me that I had yet to call in Mr Darcy's promise to explain his dislike of Mr Wickham, but there seemed to be so many matters crowding my thoughts, that I was no longer eager to hear it.

When Hannah had finished, I looked into the glass and, seeing I looked quite creditable, joined Mr Darcy for supper. I will not say our meal passed easily, but it passed reasonably. When we retired to the music room and he asked me to play for him, I did so with some pleasure. I played pieces I knew well, and when he asked me to sing, I did that, too. I had to acknowledge it was a handsome instrument, and it had always been a joy to me to lose myself in music. While my fingers danced across the keys, I need not think too much on the manner in which Mr Darcy and I had been forced to accept one another. It became an article of faith for me to make the situation between us work as well as possible, and so when he came to my bed that night, I welcomed him as I had welcomed him the previous two nights. I noticed he was freer with his kisses, and he held me longer after it was over. In the darkness, he unplaited my hair himself and asked if I would keep it free for him in the future. It stunned me to feel his fingers shaking loose my curls, but I did not protest. To my astonishment, he did not return to his bed but remained beside me, asleep. For reasons I could not fathom, this did not trouble me.

Chapter Four

My first days at Pemberley set the tone for the whole of December. In the weeks leading up to Christmas, I became acquainted with the house and its inhabitants. Hannah and I travelled to Lambton where I obtained several new gowns, and her sweet disposition made me forget the shame of having arrived with no trousseau. Mr Darcy made great efforts with me. Knowing my love of walking, he accompanied me on a number of rambles around the grounds although the snow kept us to the paths. I challenged him that he must miss his horse, and he replied that he did, but it did not signify since, as soon as the weather improved, he intended to teach me to ride. We ate our meals together, and when he worked in his study, I sat by the fire in the adjoining library and read. If he was at leisure, he joined me, and we would discuss poetry and novels we had both read. We did not discuss anything more personal, but we found common ground enough, and it was agreeable. I watched his face, lit by the orange of the fire and animated by discussion. It was hard to believe he was the same Mr Darcy who had sat in the drawing room at Netherfield and said that pride could be regulated by a "superiority of mind." I began to feel myself relax and grow comfortable. I was astonished that, on a couple of occasions, I even fell asleep in the library.

A week before Christmas, Miss Darcy returned home, accompanied by her aunt and uncle, Lord and Lady Matlock. My heart thundered as I stood with Mr Darcy watching their carriage approach, but I was determined to appear calm, and I believe I did so. I was quick to realise Hannah had been correct, and nobody had anything to fear in Miss Darcy, who, although shy, was also kind and sweet.

"Mrs Darcy." She looked flustered as her eyes met mine. "How I have longed to meet you sooner, but brother ordered me away! I have heard so much about you; I feel that it cannot be right for me to welcome you to your own house…but…it is wonderful to see you here."

"Thank you, Miss Darcy, I have longed to meet you, too, and we shall not allow your brother to keep us apart!" It did not escape me that Miss Darcy was significantly larger than I am in stature and build, and I pondered what Mr Darcy had written when he instructed Hannah to take in her gowns for me. I shot a playful look at him, which he acknowledged with a nod before continuing the introductions.

"Aunt and Uncle, Mrs Darcy. Elizabeth, Lord and Lady Matlock."

Nervous as I was, I curtseyed, smiled, and extended my hand to these august strangers who were now my family. They, in turn, were polite and affable, and I had no complaints about their company. When I went upstairs to dress for dinner, I found at my vanity a small cream box containing as fine a string of pearls as I had ever seen. Hannah informed me my husband had placed them there himself earlier in the afternoon, and he intended me to wear them that evening. I was told they were Darcy family jewels, several generations old and, if I cared to look, featured in several of the grand portraits of my predecessors that hung in the gallery. Their beauty and heaviness hung about my neck in a most unfamiliar manner, and I could hardly stop my hand from reaching up to touch them from time to time. After dinner, Mr Darcy and Lord Matlock remained in the dining room while we ladies retired to the drawing room. As soon as I was alone with Lady Matlock, I learned she, too, was a friend, not a foe.

"Well, Mrs Darcy, we have all been *desperate* to meet you, but you do not disappoint. I can see you are quite a match for Fitzwilliam, my dear."

"Thank you, Lady Matlock. I fear we must have shocked you all with the speed of our nuptials." I did not say what we all knew; the most stunning fact of all was that the new Mrs Darcy was a young woman with neither connections nor fortune. I knew I could not be what they had expected or hoped for.

"A little, a little, but it is in the manner of Fitzwilliam to be impulsive, to give us all as little warning as possible, and frankly, to do as he pleases. So, I am not vexed. Once Lord Matlock had got over his surprise, the same was true of him, and we have been greatly enjoying the time with Georgiana."

"Oh yes, Aunt, I have had a wonderful stay with you...but it is lovely to be home as well, of course, Mrs Darcy."

"It is wonderful to have you here, Miss Darcy, but you really must call me 'Elizabeth' now that we are sisters or even 'Lizzy.' That is what my own family call me although it may be a little too informal for your brother."

"Lizzy. I think it suits you greatly, and you must call me 'Georgiana.'"

Not to be left out, Lady Matlock insisted I join my husband and new sister in calling her "Aunt Mary," and so it was settled, and we were a happy party. When the men joined us, both Georgiana and I played and sang. I, however, was much embarrassed by her superior skills. The evening drifted into night, and I was well pleased with my first foray into the world of my new family.

When Mr Darcy joined me in my chamber that night, I was still at my vanity in my nightgown whilst Hannah brushed my hair. Seeing him in the mirror, she stilled her hand, curtseyed, and was gone. "Poor Hannah, you have quite frightened her away."

"I am sorry. I did not mean to disturb you. Are you ready to retire now, Elizabeth?" He touched my neck and shoulders as he said this, and his eyes seemed to bore holes into me.

"Yes, I am. Thank you, Fitzwilliam." I spoke his name naturally for the first time, and I knew he was grateful. "Thank you for allowing me to wear the pearls. They are beautiful."

"You are Mrs Darcy, Elizabeth. They are yours," he replied, turning away and drawing a deep breath. I almost gasped that he would say no more than this. Hannah had suggested to me that they had a history, and I wondered he did not wish to relate it to me or to indicate any pleasure in my wearing them as commanded. I considered, not for the first time, how different I was from my husband and how my old talkative self must be shut up and kept away from him. My lips tightened, and I looked at my reflection in the half-light.

"You have impressed my family tonight, Elizabeth. Thank you." With this, he turned, stroked my unplaited hair, led me to the bed, and said no more.

My sister Jane was my most constant correspondent, but Mama, Mary, and my friend Charlotte Lucas were only a little way behind her. My Papa did not write even after these many weeks, and I cannot say I was not a little disappointed. I pictured him sitting in his library, smiling at his book, and recalled he had never been a great letter writer. Perhaps, I had been expecting too much that he would make an exception for me. Kitty and Lydia, I assumed to be too busy chasing officers of the regiment to write to me, but otherwise, I must say I was quite flooded with letters from home. Mama wished to know about Pemberley and whether I was with child, and I feared for our poor neighbours to think how she must be showing off about my position. Mr Bingley, I was told, had not returned, and it was not known that he would. It was clear to me my poor Jane was downcast, and Christmas and the midwinter had passed in boredom and frustration for her. It was no great surprise when my sister Mary wrote to me of her engagement to Mr Collins. They were to be married from Longbourn in four weeks and then to travel to Hunsford where Mr Collins was the rector of a parish within the gift of Lady Catherine de Bourgh. I did not lament Mary's position, for I knew she was happy with it and raced to inform my husband. I found him in his study, his hand poised over some papers.

"Fitzwilliam, such news from Longbourn! Mary writes that she is engaged to Mr Collins!"

"Then I am sorry for her."

"I do not think that she requires your sympathy, Fitzwilliam. I rather think that she is happy at this turn of events. Mary takes our cousin seriously, more seriously than he is accustomed to being taken by others, and well, he could scarcely find a better wife."

"Well, in that case, I am pleased for them." His tone bespoke a man who was not at all pleased.

"The wedding is to be in Meryton in four weeks. I would think that the weather will be quite passable by then."

"I dare say."

"The journey to Hertfordshire at that time of year would probably be easier than the journey here after our . . . after we were married. I understand you would not wish to stay at Longbourn, but perchance we could lodge at the inn as you did before. What say you?"

"I think not, Elizabeth. It is a long journey, and we have not been back at Pemberley for two months. Your cousin has the living at Hunsford, and so, no doubt we will be unable to avoid him on our visit to Rosings at Easter. I see no call to travel all the way to Hertfordshire so soon."

"I see," I said confounded. "But I shall miss my sister's wedding!"

"You will see her soon enough, and a country wedding to a rector is hardly reason to go parading around the country, even for your sister."

The heat of his words prickled against my face, and my fingernails dug crescents into my palms. "She is our sister, is she not, Mr Darcy? I rather think that, were Georgiana to marry, we would not stay away."

"When Georgiana marries, she will be married from Pemberley, and she will hardly marry a man like Mr Collins."

I turned away, boiling with rage but also wounded by his having said what I knew already: that my family was a degradation to him. My mind flew to the barefaced deceit that had been used by Mama to entrap him into our marriage, and I wondered he was not less restrained in his disdain. I would not give him the satisfaction of knowing that I had spurned Mr Collins when he was available to me and I, too, had thought him ridiculous. I saw clearly now how Mr Darcy saw me, and I hated the way my feelings towards him had softened. The thought of the liberties I had allowed him, night after night, was mortifying. I missed my family so much in that moment that I could not speak. Choosing not to try, I fled the room without looking back at him.

He found me some hours later, playing duets with Georgiana, and although it was not his habit to sit in the music room during the day, he did on this occasion. My new sister and I had built up quite a repertoire, and the afternoon became an impromptu concert, however disinclined I felt to exhibit before Mr Darcy.

"Oh, Lizzy, what a wonderful partner you are! I never found such joy in playing duets before you came to Pemberley. I fancy you must have played with all your sisters."

I smiled at the thought and tried to reassure her. "I dread to think of my sisters and me in musical collaboration. No, only Mary plays, and she and I have quite different tastes." I threw a look at my husband that I hoped was not lost upon him. "You are my most favoured partner, I assure you."

The discipline of playing and turning the pages for Georgiana when she played on her own calmed me, and I came to realise that, in the first flush of unexpected happiness at Pemberley, I had been living in a dream. I had allowed myself to forget how his connection to me had been forced upon my husband and how he must lament it. Just as I had looked at Pemberley and been overwhelmed by its grandness, so he must have looked at Longbourn and found it wanting. I determined from that moment on that I would be more realistic in my attitudes.

To my surprise, he did not keep to his chamber that night. When I was already abed, he appeared in his nightclothes and stroked my blanketed arm.

"Elizabeth, are you awake?"

I rolled onto my back, staring at the hanging above and saying nothing.

"Let us not argue on this matter. I do not wish to be out of harmony with you and...I do not like to see you distressed. Of course, we would normally attend your sister's wedding, but we are to visit Rosings in April, and there you will have much time with Mary. That is only three months away, and at Rosings, there is a large house and a park for walking, as well as a parlour for taking tea with Mr Collins. Please believe me; it will be better for you. You will not be so confined or reminded of that which would be better left alone."

I knew he spoke of himself, but since he spoke kinder than he had before, I reached out to him. I thought of Mr Bingley and Jane and of how Mr Darcy could persuade him to return to her if only I could sway him.

"Of course, I know you are right. I am sorry for having been so intemperate."

THE MATTER OF MARY'S WEDDING was not mentioned between us again, and we soon fell back into step with our old habits. Mr Darcy often travelled around the estate with his steward, Mr Franks, and I busied myself with the housekeeper, Mrs Reynolds, with whom I met each morning. When he worked within doors, he did so in his study, and I often awaited him in the library where he would join me when he had finished. I was greatly surprised by how easily the hours passed in his company, but I was not romantic. His attitude regarding my sister's wedding had drawn a border between us over which I knew not to tread.

When he announced to me that Mr Bingley and his sisters were to stay at Pemberley for a week on their way to their relations in the north, I was greatly surprised. We were in my bed, and his fingers were twisting my hair. The mention of Mr Bingley's name took my mind back to the night of the Netherfield ball and smacked so of Hertfordshire and my former life. Mr Darcy, Mr Bingley, his sisters, and I had not stayed together under the same roof since Jane was taken ill at Netherfield, and we had hardly been a merry party then. Jane's absence overwhelmed me in that moment, and I longed for her to be at Pemberley, too. I knew from her letters that she still held Mr Bingley in very high esteem, and the months since his abrupt departure had passed in dullness and poor spirits. However, Mr Darcy had intimated nothing of my family being welcome, and I dared not ask to invite them.

"You are not vexed?"

"No, of course not. I look forward to seeing Mr Bingley very much. I wonder what takes him to the north. He left Netherfield so abruptly; I wonder if he shall ever return?" My husband said nothing to this.

Although I was anxious, I sought out Mrs Reynolds immediately after breakfast the next day to make arrangements for the stay of the Bingley party. We met in the library, and Mrs Reynolds appeared to have everything in hand almost before I spoke. Mr Bingley and his sisters were always accommodated in the same rooms, and they would easily be made ready in time. His favourite dish was pheasant, so that would be prepared. I could rest easy, therefore, that my being the mistress of the house would in no way diminish their enjoyment. Having settled all of this, I fancied Mr Darcy may be in his study and stepped in. I wished to see him and somehow assure him he had nothing to fear; I would handle the stay of his friends as I should.

The dimly lit, leathery room was empty, his large chair vacant, and I could tell from the smell that it had been recently cleaned—no doubt the maids taking advantage of his absence. It was a strange thing to be in there without him, and I paced the room, warmed my hands against the dying embers of the fire, and straightened some books on his desk. It was then that it caught my eye. I could not now tell you why, but it did. I sat gingerly on the edge of Mr Darcy's great chair, pulled the letter towards me, and read.

Galbraith & Company, Solicitors
65 Fleet Street, London
10 January 1813

Fitzwilliam Darcy, Esq
Pemberley, Derbyshire

Dear Mr Darcy,

I thank you for your last letter with respect to your property at Queen Anne's Gate. I have ventured to make the arrangements which you requested

of me in the most discreet manner possible and believe they are now complete.
It was not necessary for me to approach the occupant of the house, and I did
not do so, although I thank you for your advice on that matter. The title
documents are in your safe at the offices of this firm should you wish to inspect
them at any time.

I trust you are in good health. I am conscious this is a matter which you
may prefer to discuss face to face rather than by way of correspondence and if
that is the case, then I look forward to seeing you when you are next in town.

Yours sincerely,
James Galbraith

I read in confusion and astonishment. What could it mean? I knew my
husband's townhouse to be in Grosvenor Square, and he had never mentioned
another. Who was the occupant of this house in Queen Anne's Gate, and why
would Mr Darcy prefer to discuss the matter face to face than by letter? I had
a sense I was being kept in ignorance, and my heart raced with the thought
of it. Somebody had snuffed out a light in my brain, and my imagination
was falling over in the dark. I greatly feared what it *could* mean and loathed
having no real idea what it *did* mean. I resented Mr Darcy as well; he had told
me so little about himself that he had made a detective of me. If I crept about,
reading things I should not read and collecting a patchwork of half-known
things, then I blamed the man himself for his lack of openness. I had in me
the heat of knowledge that was not meant for me, and my body was a furnace.
Troubled as I was and scarcely understanding what I had read, I replaced the
letter with a shaky hand and quickly left the room. I resolved to expunge the
whole episode from my mind and make as though it had never taken place.

WHEN HANNAH ATTENDED ME THE next morning, it was apparent she was
beside herself with excitement. After my bath, she revealed all.

"Well, madam, what do you say to this?" She stepped aside, revealing a
beautiful riding habit on the bed.

"I think it is very lovely, Hannah, but I have never been fitted for it. And
as you know, I cannot ride."

"It is the master's surprise, madam. Is it not *fine*?" She stroked the fabric
and beseeched me with her eyes.

"It certainly is, Hannah. I dread to ask when I am to use it," I said, recalling that my last ride had been on a pony as a child.

"This morning, madam. The master will take you out after breakfast."

"So little time to prepare! Hannah, I feel quite betrayed by you," I said teasingly.

"Oh, madam, the master takes such care of you! I am sure he will be a kindly teacher. I do hope though . . . well, I hope that I do not say too much when I say that you should take special care."

She blinked and tilted her little, capped head. I was suddenly confused by her words and anxious, for I had come to imagine myself in a world full of secrets.

"What do you mean, Hannah?"

"Well, madam, you have not had your courses since before Christmas, so there may be a special need for care." She looked at my face searchingly. Close as we had become, she had only known me for a matter of months and did not quite have the measure of my worldliness. "It is important to avoid falling. I expect you know that."

I hardly heard her. My mind spun with the realisation that she was right and I had not even noticed.

"Have you discussed this with anyone else, Hannah?"

"Only Mrs Reynolds, madam. She asked me when you slept for so long in the library last week. I am certain she will have said nothing to anyone else."

The thought of informing my husband was my first worry, and I knew not how that could be done. So few words passed between us. I was still more discomforted by the thought of a tiny, unknown life inside me. I had forgotten my courses. In the upset surrounding Mary's engagement and the general upheaval of settling in at Pemberley, I, seemingly, had lost track of my own body.

"We cannot be sure—can we—until the child quickens?"

"No, madam."

"In that case, I shall not tell Mr Darcy just yet, but I do promise to be careful. For now, Hannah, this can be our secret." I managed a smile for her that she seemed to appreciate.

MY RIDING LESSON WAS A surprisingly joyful occasion. Mr Darcy had acquired a small, gentle grey just for me, and I named her Mrs. Wollstonecraft, which I think entertained him. Mrs. Wollstonecraft was easy to mount because of her size, but nonetheless, my husband lifted me to her saddle and rode beside me so slowly, I fancy we might have walked quicker. I had seen him riding alone, and I knew he was fast and agile.

"You are quite the instructor, Fitzwilliam. Did you teach Georgiana?"

"Our father taught Georgiana until he became ill, and then I took over the task. So I suppose we accomplished it between us. I would never want to trust either her or you to a groom when I can show you the skills myself. I know my father took the same attitude."

"And your mother—was she also a great horsewoman?"

"No, not at all. My mother did not ride. She did not enjoy outdoor pursuits as my father did. They were very different in that way. She was a great reader and spent much time indoors, often on your favourite sofa, Elizabeth." He smiled as he looked sideways at me, and I worried how many people had noted my long slumber in the library.

"Did your parents share other interests?" I asked, thinking of my own parents.

"No, I am afraid they did not. Apart from Georgiana and myself, and to an extent Pemberley, there was little that knitted them together."

"That cannot have been agreeable."

"No, it was not. But what is the past for but to learn from, Elizabeth?"

I detected in his voice a kind of sage wisdom of the spirit that I found most comforting. It pulled me towards him like bait on a fishing line. He looked at me with such intensity that I was quite overcome; and when he helped me down from Mrs. Wollstonecraft, I kissed his cheek without forethought or preamble.

Chapter Five

I began undertaking visits to tenants some weeks after arriving at Pemberley. Mama, to my knowledge, had never visited any of the Longbourn tenants, but I was aware it was customary for the wives of landed gentlemen to do so. And so, I sought both to do right and to be as my husband would expect me to be. It was a joy to step into the air, to find my way around the estate, and to begin to know the souls around me, for I am not a person to be confined. On one cold but sunny morning, I walked forth with Georgiana, each of us carrying a basket of food from the kitchens, our skirts like sails in the wind.

My new sister opened our conversation with an astonishing statement. "I cannot thank you enough, Lizzy, for marrying Fitzwilliam!"

I could not but laugh at this. "Why ever do you say that, Georgiana?"

"Well, because visiting now is not such a chore as it was before. For the past year, I had been conducting some visits with Mrs Annesley after Fitzwilliam . . . well, *suggested* that I should. He said I was old enough, the tenants would like it, and I might enjoy it. Only I did not at all! I found it very terrifying turning up at people's homes and trying to find conversation. But you, Lizzy, are such a natural. It is a much happier experience now you are here."

"Well, I am glad. But you know, Georgiana, you do not do yourself justice, for you have introduced me to all of the people we have visited and helped me to know them. You have been very helpful, dear."

I did not tell the whole truth when I said this. Georgiana had accompanied me on my visits, but for the most part, she had stood around in an awkward manner, fidgeting, and saying little. She shifted from foot to foot and nodded politely when others spoke, but she put nobody at their ease. On each visit, the sweet and easy girl who accompanied me on the journey would abandon me at the threshold and leave me to do the talking. I squeezed her arm. "You should learn to praise yourself more, Georgiana."

We laughed, and our boots grew muddy as we meandered down the eastern part of the woods towards the cottage that Mrs Reynolds had informed me was next on my rounds. "Tell me about this family, dear. What are they called? The Ashbys? What am I to expect?"

"Well, they seem very agreeable people. I have visited them a few times, and they were always very kind." With this, she fell silent, and I wondered whether Georgiana had quite grasped that it was she who was bestowing care and benevolence rather than the other way around. The more I came to know her, the less I could fathom her. She suffered an almost crippling lack of confidence and an inability to put herself before the world as the good and worthy young woman that she was. The world looked at her, and she looked away. It occurred to me it might have been her painful shyness that caused Mr Wickham to tell me she was proud. For it would be possible to assume her struggle to connect with others was borne of some idea that she was above them. Yes—that must have been his reasoning.

"I see. And, are they an old couple?"

"Oh no, they are quite young. At least, she is. Mrs Ashby is awfully pretty..."

"And do they have any children?"

"Oh yes, there were always several children present when I used to call."

"Do you know how many?"

"Oh, Lizzy, I must own I was never able to count. They were always running about so, and I am not good at discerning one small child from another. Oh dear, I am sorry. You must think me a clot!"

"I do not think that at all. We shall make a point of counting them today. Shall you help me?" She nodded and smiled bashfully. Our arms tightened against one another as the path sloped away from the wood. The bare branches of the trees formed a frame around the Ashbys' cottage, and we descended towards it. A pillar of smoke snaked from the chimney into the sky. When I knocked on the door, it was opened after a minute by a woman whose worn clothes belied her obvious youth and natural beauty.

She was heavy with child, her belly swelling under her stained apron, her back arching against the weight of it.

"Miss Darcy! And this must be the new Mrs Darcy! I am pleased to meet you, ma'am."

"And I you, Mrs Ashby."

"Come in, please, if you can abide the crowds!" She smiled at me. As she said this, a number of small faces looked at me from various corners of the room.

"Thank you, Mrs Ashby, and worry not, for I like crowds. In fact, may I be introduced to your crowd?"

"Of course, madam. Children, please come out so Mrs Darcy may see you properly. This is George, my eldest, madam. And here we have Edward, and the girls are Mary, Elizabeth, and Jane."

"I am pleased to meet you all and especially since I am an 'Elizabeth' *and* have a 'Mary' and a 'Jane' among my sisters."

We passed some time discussing the weather and the villages about before Mrs Ashby asked her elder daughter to unpack our baskets in order that we could take them back. She stroked her belly as she told me the babe was expected in the next month. I learned she had lived all her life on Pemberley land as her father had also been a tenant farmer, and her husband, William, farmed three fields to the west of the cottage. He, too, was a native of the estate.

"So we are real Pemberley people, madam. And how fortunate we are, for I'll wager you would not find a prettier spot in all England!"

Without warning, a loud and rasping cough began from behind the wall, and our hostess looked troubled. There was a moment of silence, and Georgiana looked at her lap and fiddled with her bonnet ribbons. In the end, poor Mrs Ashby was embarrassed into speaking. "Oh dear. I'm sorry, ma'am, that is my William—Mr Ashby, I mean. He has had trouble with his chest, ma'am, and so he has been resting. I…would you mind if I just attended to him for a moment?"

"No, no, of course not. Please do!" I hoped she took from my smile that I did not mind being left for a few minutes, but I could not be sure. Worry was carved upon her pretty face as she moved into the next room. Georgiana, who had been sitting next to me, smiling and nodding with verve, informed me in a whisper that Mr Ashby had never been at home when she had called in the past. We then sat for some time in the darkened room, saying little, smiling at the children, and trying not to listen to Mr Ashby's hacking and spluttering. When Mrs Ashby re-emerged, she was flustered, and knowing she would never suggest we should depart, I anticipated her.

"Mrs Ashby, thank you very much for your hospitality, but Miss Darcy and I would not trespass further on you. So we shall bid you farewell and shall certainly visit again soon."

"I am sorry you have to go, but thank you for your visit and for the baskets. We are very grateful. We really are."

"I know, I know…" I hesitated then, for I had not been a gentleman's wife long enough to know the form in such situations. Should I go and leave this poor family to their privacy or ought I to enquire further? After some moments of indecision, my native inquisitiveness got the better of me. "Mrs Ashby, I hope that Mr Ashby shall soon be well. How long has he been troubled by his chest?"

"Well, it must be about a month now, ma'am. It was a harsh winter, and I have wondered what that did for his chest. He has always been prone to a cough."

"And has he seen anyone about it?"

"No, no, madam. I am sure there is no need for that. He shall be fine, but thank you so much for your kind words."

With that, we shook hands with Mrs Ashby and, at my instigation, with each of the children. The tiny front door was closed upon them, and Georgiana and I, arm in arm, empty baskets on each side and the wind at our backs, made for Pemberley. On the way, I mithered about how best to assist the Ashbys since they were obviously in great need of help. I did not wish to have to approach either Fitzwilliam or his steward, Mr Franks, on the matter. Mr Franks was a stern, gentlemanlike man and not approachable at all. I wondered, not for the first time, whether old Mr Wickham had been a more friendly prospect when *he* was the steward. Given the ease and agreeable nature of his son, it was hard to think he can have been any different. I pictured an older Mr Wickham, greying slightly at the temples and lined around the eyes, and imagined I would have liked him very much. As it was, I did not wish to deal with Mr Franks, so after luncheon, I called for Mrs Reynolds.

"You asked to see me, madam?" The door to my sitting room clicked shut behind her.

"Ah yes, thank you, Mrs Reynolds. I have been visiting the Ashbys at Haddon today, and I am rather worried about them. Mr Ashby has an appalling cough, and I rather think he would benefit from being seen by a physician. I would like to arrange this and, of course, pay for it. I am sure I can pay for it from my pin money. But are you able to arrange it?"

"Yes, madam, of course. But I am sure you do not need to pay for it from your pin money. I can speak to Mr Franks about it, but I am sure estate funds are normally used for that sort of thing."

I thought of confiding in her, of trusting her with my inhibitions, and on balance, I preferred to keep them to myself. "There is no need to trouble him, Mrs Reynolds. I am happy to pay for it, and I rather think the Ashbys may be embarrassed to think of everyone here knowing this charity had been given. As it is, it shall just be between us, and I think that may be better."

"Erm, well, if you are sure, madam. I can arrange for Dr Worthing to call. He lives in Lambton, and I can write to him today. Will that be acceptable?"

"Yes, I think that will do very well. I do hope she shall not be offended at my having taken this step, but he did sound very bad, and she is very heavy with child herself, Mrs Reynolds, with five young ones already born. She has a great deal to worry on. I hope I do not add to it."

That evening after supper, Georgiana retired early to bed with a headache and left Mr Darcy and me in the music room. Anticipating he would like me to play, I opened the instrument and began a simple, easy piece I knew by heart.

"I do not wonder that Georgiana has a headache; it was very windy on our way back from Haddon today. We were nearly blown back to Pemberley."

"But you are well, Elizabeth? I hope you are not ill as well."

"No, not at all. I am fine. I have been enjoying the tenant visits very much. I love to step outside, learn my way around, and meet the people who live here. It makes me feel as though I know where I am. Do you understand that, sir?"

He looked at me steadily. "Yes, I think I do. How did you find the Ashbys?"

"Oh, not well at all. Mrs Ashby appears to be a very agreeable woman, but I can scarce imagine how she copes. She has five children, all of them less than six years of age and another expected in a month. Her husband, I believe, is ill. He was there, but we saw him not. He was coughing appallingly in another room, and his chest sounded very bad."

"Is that why you have asked about Dr Worthing visiting?"

I wondered whether he was challenging or simply asking. His tone, as was often the case, was a mystery to me. I was ready to defend myself. "Yes, it is. I believe he needs a doctor. It is not a cold, Fitzwilliam. It sounded dreadful. I was glad we had taken two baskets instead of just one. But I fear they are in crisis. Both of the Ashbys have lived all of their lives on Pemberley land. They are Pemberley people. I took the view we ought to be doing more than we were for them." I looked at his handsome, inscrutable face and added quietly, "I hope I did right."

I hated begging for his blessing thus. In my heart, I added that poor Mr Wickham was a Pemberley person as well, born and raised here, and he should never have been abandoned as he has been. I wondered how Mr Darcy could justify to himself that he had treated his father's godson so shabbily.

"Of course you did, Elizabeth. I was not suggesting you had done anything wrong. I...you are doing very well. I do not believe you were ever taught how to be the mistress of a great estate. There is no reason to think you would have been. Your parents can hardly have envisaged this for you, so you are relying on Mrs Reynolds and your native abilities. But I hope you know that...well, I do not find anything wanting."

As he spoke, I was heating with frustration and wounded pride. The piece I was playing reached its conclusion, and my hands rested lightly in the middle of the instrument. I wondered what he expected me to say to this little speech. Ought I to kiss his feet for having raised me in the world? Ought I to offer that I never need write my parents, as well as never see them, since their condition in life is so far below his? Could I ever repay the condescension he had shown in marrying me?

"No, I am not complaining, Elizabeth. I was merely concerned that you told Mrs Reynolds you would use your pin money rather than estate funds. There is no need for that. That sort of thing ought to be paid for from the estate. Your pin money is for you to spend on yourself."

"I did not want everyone to know, that is all. Mrs Ashby seemed... well, I thought she would not appreciate it if everybody here knew about their plight; I could pay out of my pin money, and only Mrs Reynolds and I would know about it. To get money from the estate, I would have to approach Franks and who knows who else. As it is, Mrs Reynolds clearly went straight to you after having spoken to me, so I need not have bothered.

I did not know she was so little to be trusted."

I tried not to be wounded by the suggestion that I had betrayed my inferior background by the manner in which I had tried to help the Ashbys. I wanted to say it was not ignorance. I wanted to say it was not ostentatious charity that motivated me, just a desire to assist them in the best and most discreet way. I wanted to but did not. Images of the swollen belly of Mrs Ashby and echoes of her husband's hacking cough whirred around my mind. I flushed to think Mr Darcy thought my lack of preparation for being the mistress of Pemberley was so obvious, and I stared down at my fingers resting on the black and white keyboard. For a few moments, he spoke though I did not hear him. "...if you are too tired to play, we can retire. Would you like to retire?"

"Erm, I am sorry I was wool gathering. Yes, I can play if you like, or we can retire. I don't mind, Fitzwilliam."

He approached me and stroked my shoulder, his fingers sliding slightly below the silk of my sleeve. He was my husband, and yet, I was shocked by the intimacy of it.

"No, you look fatigued. Let us to bed?"

We did go to bed, and as had become customary—and with little conversation—he made love to me. In the months of our marriage, I had become well used to the patterns and rhythms of the act. I knew where on his back he liked to be stroked and how to recognise the beginning, the middle, and the end. I knew he liked my hair about my shoulders, and I took care that he found me in such a pose when he came to me. I met the kisses he bestowed upon me with kisses of my own. When he pushed my nightgown up to bunch around my waist, I looked into his eyes and smiled. In all of this, I told myself I acted out of my determination that our marriage should work as well as may be—work as well as any union between two strangers thrown together by circumstance might work. But in the darkness of my chamber, when I was in his embrace, I knew that was no longer quite explanation enough. My feelings had changed, despite my loyalty to my family and friends at home and my own better judgement. Being with him night after night, feeling his skin and strength and breath had touched me, and I wanted it for itself.

On this occasion, he rolled off me and pulled me into a tight embrace.

"Elizabeth, I hope you did not think I disapproved of you sending a physician to Ashby?"

I stared at his bare neck and placed my small hands against his chest. It was shaming that his physical closeness had so tempered my attitude towards him, but it was true. "Well, I do not know. I could not make out what you thought really. I suppose, I feared you did disapprove, or that you might."

"I do not at all. It was the right thing to do. We cannot let people on our land suffer in silence, and well…for his family's sake, we must do all we can for him. No, I could not approve of simply leaving him to the care of Mrs Ashby, especially in her condition. You did what I would have done if visiting fell to me."

I considered his words, and they being by his standards a compliment, I resolved to accept them as such. My hands stroked his chest.

"I am glad, Fitzwilliam. Your approval is rarely given, I believe, so more worth the earning. Thank you."

Chapter Six

Three days before we expected the Bingley party, we attended a ball given by our neighbour, Lady Bellamy. The Bellamy estate, Standenton Park, bordered the Pemberley Woods, and I had glimpsed it on my walks through tangled branch and bracken. Now, our carriage clattered towards it on the open path of its approach, and I was breathless with anticipation. It was the first time I had accompanied my husband in company outside our home, and I knew it would not do to let him down or appear less than I should be. His smile, which he turned on me as he had assisted me into the carriage at Pemberley, drove me on in my ambition to please him. Unconsciously, I fingered the Darcy pearls that hung about my neck.

"I hope you are not concerned about this event, Elizabeth. I am sure it will pass quite easily, and Lord and Lady Matlock will be there."

"Yes, I look forward to seeing them very much. And besides, it is not in my nature to fear a ball. I am desirous to meet with my neighbours, and I do love to dance." I thought of his unwillingness to dance in Hertfordshire, of his solemn face circling the company, and the ladies hoping in vain to be asked. "I hope you will not wish to sit out *all* of the dances? For then nobody will ask me, and I should not wish to be taken for an invalid."

"I am not a great fan of large gatherings, and as for dancing, well, a little goes a long way. But I am sure we can dance a little, you and I."

"Is that your manner of asking me to dance, sir?" I asked boldly. "Should you not be more specific? Should you not reserve certain dances? That would have the advantage of certainty for us both. Or do you assume, sir, that nobody else will ask me and I will, therefore, be available at your pleasure?"

"I am sorry, Elizabeth. I did not realise I had to *ask* my wife as I would an ordinary acquaintance. But since you wish it, would you do me the honour of dancing the first with me, Mrs Darcy?"

Having obtained the offer for which I had been worrying at him for days, I was quite undone by the twinkle in his eyes as he smiled at me. Unequal as I was to responding with a witty remark, I smiled back and thanked him.

"As for our neighbours, I hope you are not disappointed, Elizabeth. I believe Lady Bellamy has invited most of the county, so you can expect a fair amount of farming talk. Apart from my aunt and uncle, I know not who will be present, but we can expect all of our near neighbours and many other families besides."

"It is a shame Georgiana cannot attend. I believe she felt it keenly, waving us goodbye at the door."

"There will be time enough for balls when she is out in society. She is too young to be out, and she is much better off at home."

His tone told me he would brook no argument, but I thought of my sisters, all out in company at fifteen, and I was doubtful. My view was that Georgiana would benefit from a little more society and her painful shyness was, in part, a consequence of Fitzwilliam preventing her from ever meeting anyone outside of her family. She would benefit, surely, from some more society. I thought this but did not say it.

The home of Lord and Lady Bellamy was a splendid one indeed, and they welcomed us with smiles and happy words. The event was far larger than I had anticipated, and great crowds of people seemed to push around me. Fans fluttered, skirts swished, jewelled heads bobbed, and the energy of being there swept through me. My husband seemed concerned, firstly, that others should not brush against me in their eagerness to reach the ballroom, and secondly, that we should locate Lord and Lady Matlock without delay. His head craned around the room, his gaze passing over one hundred tailcoats and coiled hair arrangements until, at last, he rested his search.

"Elizabeth, Darcy, what a joy this is! But there are too many people!"

"I agree, Aunt Mary," said Fitzwilliam, bowing to her. "I had no idea that Bellamy had invited the families of three counties. It is quite stifling in here, and the dancing has not yet begun!"

"Can there be too many people at a ball?" I asked. "Does a large number not simply assure those of us whose husbands are not given to dancing that we shall not be in want of a partner?" I squeezed his arm, and Lady Matlock laughed.

"I have asked you for the first dance, Elizabeth. Is there to be no end to this merrymaking?" he said, raising his eyebrows slightly. His eyes creased as he smiled at me, and I felt a sudden lurch in my belly that took me quite unawares. For a moment, I was made speechless by his attention towards me, but I battled hard to regain my composure.

"Certainly not, sir!"

I had not noticed when I danced with Fitzwilliam at Netherfield how elegant he appeared in a ballroom, but I noticed it now. We touched and parted to the pattern of the dance, and I admired his handsome form in the unusual setting of a crowd for the first time. The music reached its peak, completed, and the dance was at an end. I gladly accepted Fitzwilliam's arm, and he led me from the floor, I assumed back to his aunt and uncle. We had made little progress when we were interrupted by a lady's voice.

"Mr Darcy! I thought that I spied you from across the room. How marvellous to see you again, sir. And this must be Mrs Darcy!"

The statuesque and exquisitely dressed figure of a woman appeared before me, and though she accosted us assertively, there was a strange, buzzing, nervousness in her manner. Her hands seemed to wave around unnecessarily as she spoke, and she flicked the luscious, dark curls framing her handsome face. There was, I fancied, mischief there but also anxiety. She sported a pearl bracelet around her narrow wrist with which she fidgeted. She was young, no older I would hazard than myself, and she had a gentleman in tow, half a pace behind her. An emotion I could not place swept across Fitzwilliam's face.

"Mrs Woodham, it is a pleasure, and Mr Woodham. May I introduce Mrs Darcy? " Bows met curtseys, and smiles were exchanged, but I was none the wiser.

"You are far from home, Mr Woodham. You must have travelled fifty miles to be here." Fitzwilliam turned to me and said, "Mr and Mrs Woodham live at Pittleworth, which is to the north of Pemberley, Elizabeth."

With that, Mrs Woodham and Mr Woodham spoke at once: the wife to suggest we must be their guests and Mr Woodham to say Mrs Woodham wished to attend and that her wish was his command. They both seemed to me to be pushing themselves forward in a remarkable manner. There was an odd and mercifully short silence before Mrs Woodham turned to address me.

"I understand you are lately married, Mrs Darcy. So am I. Mr Woodham and I have only been married these two weeks—imagine that!"

"Well, yes, I am. Mr Darcy and I were married in December. This is my first visit to Standenton Park. Are you a frequent visitor here?"

"Oh no, I have never been here before, but Mr Woodham knows the Bellamys, and I believe he has been here several times. It is lovely, is it not? I lived in London before I married, so I am learning country ways, Mrs Darcy."

I wondered whether her forwardness was partly attributable to this and resolved to think kindly of her. She took my arm, closing her beautiful jewelled hand around the lace of my sleeve before continuing. "I have heard, Mrs Darcy, that you sing and play beautifully; is that true? I should love to hear it."

"Well, not beautifully at all, but I do enjoy music very much."

"Shall we hear you tonight? I should like that very much. I love to hear a good song, but I am not talented myself. My sister, Sophia, is a wonderful pianist. I believe she has all of the musical talent in our family!"

"Well, I shall play if requested, but I would not wish to excite your anticipation, for I am no virtuoso. I play very undemanding pieces really. Wherever did you hear of my playing?"

She appeared shocked by this simple and reasonable question, but as she opened her mouth to speak, we were interrupted by Mr Woodham. "Alice, you never lose an opportunity to promote your sister's talents! She is superb at the pianoforte, Mrs Darcy, but for myself I cannot better the majesty of an orchestra. If I should play an instrument, I should play the violin and be one among many!"

We laughed lightly at the idea, and within moments, Mr Woodham asked me to dance the next with him. It would have been unthinkable to refuse. Fitzwilliam was clearly acquainted with him. In any event, he was a polite and amiable young man, and I could see no evil in it. To the soft harmony of the strings, we danced. We threaded and bobbed our way through the routine, smiling to other partners, and being reunited, laughed with one another. Though charming and pleasant, he did not quite hold my attention. Before long, my eyes wandered across the floor, taking in courting couples and spinsters sitting out the dance.

The sight of the *two of them* talking struck me like an axe to the spine.

Mrs Woodham and Fitzwilliam stood where we had left them, heads inclined towards one another, eyes locked, lips jittering in speech as if nobody else were present. They were neither touching nor improperly close, but I could feel in my bones an odd and indefinable intimacy emanating from them. She looked upon my husband, not as an indifferent acquaintance, but as one who really knew him, and the sight of it hounded me. How it could be that so young a woman, raised in town, engaged my husband so, I knew not. A wild feeling of resentment built up inside me. I began to feel giddy.

"How do you find Pemberley, Mrs Darcy?" interjected my partner, seeming to sense my distraction.

"It is wonderful, Mr Woodham. It is quite the most wondrous setting I could imagine. I scarcely know what I have done to deserve it. Are you familiar with Pemberley yourself?"

We parted, smiled at others, and were reunited.

"Well, a little. I visited there with my parents many years ago when old Mr Darcy and Lady Anne were alive, but I recall little of it. I understand it is a very splendid estate." His words seemed to hang in the air between us, and I believe he expected something from me by way of comment. But I knew not what to give, so I simply danced and pondered the connection between his wife and my husband until I felt quite poorly.

By the time my dance with Mr Woodham was completed, I had calmed. I forced myself to do so. I reasoned that, as Fitzwilliam could not know all about me, I could not know all about him. I had no right to be so affronted. We had not married, after all, for love. There was nothing improper in being acquainted with a young woman who was the wife of an acquaintance. He had maintained throughout our conversation his customary attention to me, and I had no complaint. As Mr Woodham escorted me back to him at the end of the dance, I consoled myself thus.

Mrs Woodham, upon our returning, almost threw herself at her husband's person and demanded a dance. He was willing to give it, and they were gone. As they scampered towards the dance floor like children, Fitzwilliam was silent at my side.

"Mr and Mrs Woodham seem a very friendly couple, Fitzwilliam. Are you well acquainted with them?"

"Erm, no, not well acquainted. Woodham's father hunted with mine, and they have a good estate. He has been to Pemberley but not for some

years." He paused, his eyes fixed straight ahead of him. "I was surprised to
see them here."

He said no more, and I, fearful of what answers there may be, ventured
no questions. We were soon joined by Lord and Lady Matlock, and the remainder of the evening was lost in dances and pleasant conversation. I danced
once more with Fitzwilliam and with Lord Matlock and with our host. But
otherwise, I sat with my husband, conversing with his relations and nursing
my cup of punch. My reverie was broken only once as I returned from the
dance floor on the arm of my husband's uncle. Through the crowd of couples
and laughing faces, I spied my husband and his aunt, apparently arguing.
Her expression was most fierce, and her hands shook in exclamation as she
spoke. Her greying curls jittered below the feathers of her headpiece. His own
face, I knew, bespoke irritation. Whatever could they be disagreeing about?
I was overcome with the sense that I was in ignorance of some great matter.

Later, darkness filled the sky like spilled ink, the air grew chilly, and
'twas time to leave. I drew my cloak about me and felt my slipper slide
slightly on the icy surface of the iron step as I entered our carriage. I saw
my breath on the air in the tiny light from the lamps outside. Otherwise,
it was all darkness, and I felt along the frozen leather seat with my gloved
hand before sitting on it. Mr Darcy immediately began bundling my legs
with a further blanket and then sat beside me, his arm wrapped about me.

"I am sorry about this cold, Elizabeth. We should have departed before
the night became so chilled."

Our frosty breaths met and mingled in the enclosed space of the carriage.
"It shall not matter, sir. We shall soon be warm, and Pemberley is not far.
The dancing was worth the cold." I smiled at him in what I hoped was a
winsome manner, and he gave a guarded smile back.

If he had only spoken some words of affection and reassurance, I would
not have pressed him. I longed to be in his confidence and to be trusted with
his true, unvarnished thoughts. But words, he gave me none. The spectre
of how little I knew him and his history stirred within me. The memory
of Mrs Woodham playing with her bracelets and looking at my husband
with knowing eyes appeared to me as we drove on in the darkness. It was
like an itch I could not but scratch. We were hardly outside the gates of
Standenton Park when I was worrying at him for knowledge and goading
him into an argument.

"I enjoyed my dance with Mr Woodham. He seems a pleasant young man. I wonder you have never mentioned them."

"Well, they are not close neighbours, Elizabeth. I was surprised to see them there at all."

"I wonder you did not ask Mrs Woodham to dance while I was engaged with Mr Woodham, Fitzwilliam. I do not think she would have been a punishment to stand up with."

I endured the silence for a moment to see whether he would fill it, and just as I began to give up hope, he sighed, removed his arm from around me, and said, "You know that I am not a great dancer, and I do not enjoy prancing from partner to partner. One of the advantages of being married is that I am now less subject to the aspirations of every woman in the ballroom."

These last words were spoken sharply and unkindly. My mama's behaviour at Netherfield and afterwards had shocked me to the core, but to suggest that *I* had been out to ensnare him was an outrageous insult *and* completely untrue. "Perhaps you do yourself too much credit, sir. I can assure you that, if it is Netherfield of which you speak, I had no aspirations of the kind, and I hope you were not excessively troubled by the notion that I did."

"I was not talking about Netherfield. And if you recall, I asked *you* to dance with me on that occasion of my own volition. *You* did not throw yourself in my way by way of seeking a dance. It should be obvious that I am sparing in my approach to dancing, and I would only ever ask a woman with whom I was acquainted."

"But you are acquainted with Mrs Woodham!"

"Only on the basis that she is married to Woodham. In any case, Elizabeth, why on earth are you so concerned at my not having asked Mrs Woodham to dance? You have only this evening been introduced to her, and quite by chance."

"But you must have known her before she was married, Fitzwilliam, for she has only been Mrs Woodham these two weeks."

He drew in his breath, and in the darkness threw his head back. His eyes were closed, and the skin around his mouth tightened slightly. I could not see these things in the dimness of the carriage, but I knew them to be true.

"May I ask to what these questions tend?"

"Merely to the illustration of these acquaintances and your relations with them. I am trying to make them out."

"And dare I ask your conclusions?"

"Oh, I do not get on at all, Fitzwilliam. For example, I see you with the Woodhams, and they seem to know you well, including Mrs Woodham, who is married for only two weeks and is not a native of Derbyshire. But you say little of them, if anything. Before tonight, I had never heard of them. Now, when I ask, you have little you are willing to tell. And so you see, I am puzzled exceedingly."

"Well, maybe you would do better not to worry about such a trifling matter," he grumbled loudly. "There is nothing to be said about the Woodhams, Elizabeth, and that is why I do not do so. They are a young couple with whom I am slightly acquainted, and I have nothing else to say about them."

The remainder of our journey home passed in an uneasy silence. Trees, hedges, dry stone walls, and low cottages flew past the carriage windows in greys and blacks. In the torment of my mood, I fancied them all tombstones. The racket of the carriage and the whinnying of the horses were the only sounds, for my husband and I each watched the cold night whistling by and said nothing. I knew that I should not have pushed him, that I should not have ended a pleasant evening with discord, and that the light was not really worth the candle. At the same time, I resented his lack of openness with me. Did I not deserve some honesty? Did I not deserve some words of affection?

Chapter Seven

The next morning was wet and chilly, and I quickly resigned myself to a day spent within doors. I re-read my latest letters from Hertfordshire and penned my replies. For Mama, I included details of the ball, although none of the ones that most concerned me. I knew she should like to hear of thronging ballrooms in grand houses and fashionable dresses, so that is what I told her. To Jane, I wrote far more of our life within Pemberley, of my walks and reading, and of my adventures on Mrs Wollstonecraft. I decided not to reveal we were expecting Mr Bingley and his sisters in but a few days. It was clear from Jane's words that Mr Bingley's absence had caused her great melancholy, and I did not wish to exacerbate it. I fancied myself an agent of Jane's interest, and I decided to find out what I could of that gentleman's feelings before exciting Jane's expectations. I wanted my letters to comfort her, not to worry her into a state of nervous anxiety. I did not mention to either Mama or Jane my suspicions of being with child. I told myself that, not having informed Mr Darcy, it would be wrong to tell others. However, I knew in my heart that there was more to it. The idea that I may have a child was a matter of such importance and so overwhelming, I did not know how to say it. I feared that, by proclaiming it, I would unleash something too great before it was necessary. And so, in cowardice, I kept it to myself.

This correspondence done, I was overwhelmed by fatigue and wearily took myself to my chamber where I climbed atop my bed and promptly fell asleep. When I awoke, it was to see Mr Darcy sitting in a chair beside the bed, reading some letters.

"Elizabeth, I am worried about all of this sleeping during the day. Are you quite well?" he asked as he saw me begin to stir.

"Yes, I am well. I think the ball must have tired me. I am fine. Thank you for being concerned." I added the last by way of a peace offering after our argument in the carriage. He did not seem to understand and answered me sharply.

"You do not need to thank me for being concerned for you. But if you are ill, then you should say so."

I thought better of continuing this discussion and called for tea, which Hannah brought to my bedside in very short order. I poured Mr Darcy a cup, but he did not leap to drink it.

"Am I right, sir, that you are not fond of tea?"

"Yes, I am not as fond as some. I believe you are?"

"Yes. I am."

"And you find this to your taste, I hope?"

My tongue lingered on my answer. "Yes." The inanity of our discussion at that moment threatened to engulf me. I knew, despite myself, that I loved him. I loved him for reasons I could not name and much to my surprise. I loved him and needed to be loved in return. When it had started and where it had come from, I knew not. It would seem I was in the middle before I knew that I had begun. And yet, I felt misery and frustration that between us we could manage nothing better than a discussion of tea. I, who could converse well with anyone, had been bested by Mr Darcy when I desired his good conversation more than that of any other. In my desperation to discuss something meaningful, I surprised myself with my forwardness.

"Tell me about Mr Wickham."

He turned to me with a start. "Wickham? What has brought this on?"

"Nothing, but I would like to know why you have such a low view of him, and, well, you did promise me that you would explain. Do you remember?"

He coughed and looked about him. "Yes. What do you want to know?"

"There is no need to be ill-tempered about it. I am interested in how you came to dislike him. That is all."

"Well, if you insist, Elizabeth. But I hope you shall not have need to know that George Wickham is a man to be avoided. I very much hope you shall not be troubled by him again."

"Yes, I doubt I shall ever see him again, for how could our paths cross?

You may call it historical interest if you will, Fitzwilliam. But I would still like to know. Especially since, if I am right, you were trying to tell me when ... "
I paused and looked down at my hands. I did not feel equal to mentioning the Netherfield ball, and so I did not. "I believe that you may have tried to tell me before. You promised me, and so, yes, I do wish to know."

"Very well. I hardly know where to begin ... because ... of course, I do not know what he has said to you. But maybe it is for the best that you do not tell me."

With this, he stood abruptly and took a noisy breath. I sat in silence as he paced to the fireplace and leaned against it; the light of the flame flickered against his profile.

"George Wickham is the son of my father's steward, who was an excellent man and very well respected hereabouts. He was greatly missed when he died about ten years ago. My father was Wickham's godfather and had always taken a great interest in him. He provided for him to be educated as a gentleman, and to my father's eyes, he always appeared to be very much thriving on it. For myself, I was once very close to George. We played together as boys, and I considered him a friend—at times, almost a brother. But as we grew older, we grew apart. Being the same age, we went up to Cambridge in the same term, but there our lives diverged dramatically. By that time, George Wickham's habits were as dissolute as his manners were engaging and well—I cannot tell you the details, Elizabeth. But suffice to say, neither his father nor mine would have been proud of the way in which he conducted himself when far from home. In any case, it transpired that his father was not long for the world, and after he died, my own father took George even more under his wing. He had long intended George for the church, taking the view that it was an ideal occupation for an educated man of no fortune. George went along with this idea, although he and I knew how unsuited he was. When five years ago my father died, his will provided, as we all expected, that George should be entitled to the living at Kympton as soon as it fell vacant. My heart was heavy as I knew he would be a poor guide to his flock, but there it was. It was my father's wish, and I could see no way forward but to honour it. As it turned out, however, George had other ideas and disavowed any interest at all in the church or the parish. He requested and he was granted the sum of three thousand pounds in place of the living. He expressed an interest in studying the law. I hoped rather than believed him to be in earnest, and I handed him a cheque for the agreed sum, praying some good would come of it. What he did with the funds and how he lived, I knew not..."

He looked at me and then looked away, his eyes seemingly searching for some missing thing. He clenched his fists and exhaled. His body was tense, and his face was troubled. I nodded, hoping to reassure him, and he moved towards me. Our tea by this time was quite cold, and I leaned over, touching his hand with mine as he drew near.

"Yes?"

"I knew not. I did not expect to see him again, and I was shocked that he surfaced in Meryton with the militia. I assume he squandered the money I conferred on him, for there is no other reasonable conclusion."

He stopped, and his silence told me he had reached the end of his tale. I knew in my bones that he was in earnest. It was a shock to realise I did not question his honesty. I thought of Mr Wickham's willingness to be-smirch Fitzwilliam upon his first meeting with me, and I also thought of his avoidance of meeting him at Netherfield. The remembrance of scanning the Netherfield ballroom upon my arrival, longing for a dance with Mr Wickham, came back to me, and I was greatly ashamed. I had been a fool. I had judged a man—two men—at great speed, with little thought, and quite incorrectly. Fitzwilliam's revelations to me seemed to have given him no comfort. He looked about in a distracted manner, and there was stress in his face and hands.

"Now, I understand. Thank you for telling me." I took a great risk and kissed his head, for which I was rewarded with a pale smile and an odd look.

But just as I thought he might kiss me in return, he stood and said, "I shall leave you now, Elizabeth," then bolted from the room like a rabbit from a trap.

Chapter Eight

The next day was a fine one, so I set out to visit the Ashbys. Hannah accompanied me, and together we trudged through the woods with baskets of plenty from the Pemberley kitchens. Being a native of Derbyshire, an excellent walker, and a long-term servant to the Darcys, she knew all the best routes and which parts of the path were less slippery after rain. As the cottage appeared before me, I found I had enjoyed her company so much that I hardly registered that we had walked for an hour to get there. I knocked upon the door in good spirits, hopeful that the visit of Dr Worthing, which I knew to have been the week before, had been helpful. After some little wait, the door was answered by young George.

"Good morning, George. Is your Mama at home?"

He gulped and stared at Hannah, seemingly lost for words. His big eyes looked about the room, and he appeared to be on the verge of shutting the door on us when a great screaming cry issued from within. Hannah knelt to meet his eyes.

"George, do not be afraid. Is that your mama? Where is she, my lovey?"

"She's abed miss," he said, pointing at the little door on the other side of the room.

With that, and not a little trepidation, Hannah and I sprang into the cottage and, knocking lightly, entered the other room. There was but one tiny window, and although it was only early spring, it felt hot within. The place was modest, and the air dank. My eyes struggled to focus in the dimness. A simple bed stood in the middle of the room on a hard wooden floor, and upon it was Mrs Ashby. Kneeling with her arms outstretched and her head hanging down, she groaned, roared, and let out odd sounds quite unlike speech. She appeared to me as an animal caged in the tiny room. She looked up at the light from the door and, seeing me, appeared to be horrified. "Mrs Darcy!" Having said this, she gasped and seemed to lose the power of speech altogether.

Hannah rapidly took charge. "George, you understand your Mama's time is come, don't you? Do you know who usually assists her?"

"Old Mrs Cutler, miss, from over Alderedge way. Edward is running there now, miss."

"And where is your papa, George?"

"He is out in the fields, miss."

"Thank you, George." Hannah patted his fair head as she stood to face me.

"Madam, it is only three miles to Alderedge, so hopefully, Mrs Cutler should be here anon . . ."

"Hannah, have you . . . been present at an event like this before?"

"Yes, madam. I have helped to birth a baby more than once for my sisters. Is it the first time that you have seen—" She paused, not knowing how to continue.

"Yes, it is." I gulped to think of the significance of the thing before me. "I have never seen a woman labouring in my life."

I was struck with fear to look upon Mrs Ashby, her body pinned to the bed like a crab, and her face contorted in agony. However, I knew we could not possibly leave her with only the children in the hope this Mrs Cutler may arrive before the event. We were told Edward would inform his father on his way home from Mrs Cutler, but we did not expect or desire Mr Ashby should attend his wife himself. Either Hannah or I could walk back to Pemberley for help, but the round journey would be lengthy, and the other one would be left alone with Mrs Ashby.

"Hannah, we must both stay at least until this Mrs Cutler gets here —maybe longer. You seem to know what you are doing, so you are in charge. What must I do to help?"

Hannah smiled sweetly, relieved of suggesting that role reversal herself. We set about making Mrs Ashby more comfortable by rubbing the small of her back and tying her long hair up. Between pains, she gasped that I should sit in the parlour, that Mrs Cutler would arrive soon, and that she was ashamed to be putting me to so much trouble. I bid her not to worry and got on with the jobs Hannah had given me. I wondered what Mr Darcy would make of me laying cloths upon Mrs Ashby's hot head and keeping her company at such a time. His disapproval—I knew—was a risk I had to take. All I could do was to try to be useful and not to become too fearful of what may be in store for me. Hannah was calm and competent and did not appear to be afraid. What straits poor Mrs Ashby would have been in if I had been visiting with Georgiana for company!

After one of the pains seemed to decline and Mrs Ashby had calmed, Hannah spoke directly to her. "Mrs Ashby, while you are quiet, I am going to check on you. Do you think we can get you on your back?"

I could not have understood less had she been speaking a foreign tongue, but Mrs Ashby appeared to be in collusion with these odd expressions and began with Hannah's assistance to roll onto her back. Her legs lay akimbo like those of a sleeping dog. It was a great shock to me when Hannah crouched down at the end of the bed and thrust her hand up Mrs Ashby's skirts. The poor lady closed her eyes and looked to the side, but otherwise she did not appear to be distressed by this invasive procedure.

"You are getting there, Mrs Ashby, but you may have a while yet. We shall keep you comfortable, and you must keep going. Can you do that?"

Her red face nodded, and she murmured, "Yes." She was about to speak more but was overtaken by pain and let out a great thundering shriek. I looked about me and wondered how I should bear such pain myself. Matters seemed to continue thus for an eternity, the light changing within the house as the day progressed. Shadows crept across the unadorned walls, and the children were heard to come and go and shuffle about in the next room. I sat beside Mrs Ashby, allowing her to squeeze my hand during her pains and promising her the children were all perfectly fine in the parlour. When circumstances allowed, Hannah and I assisted Mrs Ashby to strip down to her shift. Her dress, I folded and placed on a lonely looking chair by the side of the bed. I observed that the agony seemed to creep up on her and build to a crescendo for a minute before declining, giving the poor creature a moment of peace. I had just begun to feel I knew the pattern of things when they changed radically.

Hannah, upon pushing her hand up Mrs Ashby's shift for a second time, pronounced she was "open" and asked her, "Do you feel ready to push?" The young woman gave an emphatic, scarlet-faced, and loud, "Yes."

I tried to appear as though I knew what was taking place, but I was lost. Hannah then enlisted me in pulling the lady back over to her front where she crouched, hands and knees upon the bed.

"Madam, if you do not want to be present at this part, I can manage on my own. Maybe you would prefer to sit in the parlour?"

I thought mayhap she had seen the dread upon my face and was trying to spare me the sight of the babe leaving its mother's body. I thought of the child within my belly, and a strange determination rose within me. "No, Hannah, I shall stay. Just tell me what I must do."

"Very well, Mrs Darcy. If you could sit at Mrs Ashby's head and talk to her in an encouraging way, I shall guide the babe out."

Thus, we proceeded. I perched myself beside Mrs Ashby's head and, placing my hand on hers, informed her she was doing very well and should continue. Periodically, Hannah would command the lady to "push," and her face would redden, and its muscles tighten. I knew not how much time passed, only that something momentous was proceeding at a speed and rhythm of its own. From my position, I could not see beyond the curtain of her shift that divided one end of Mrs Ashby from the other. So, it was a surprise to me when Hannah announced that she could see the baby's head. The temperature in the tiny room had soared, and Mrs Ashby's straining and groaning increased in strength. Her noises, Hannah's commands, and even my whispered words seemed to escalate in volume.

"The head's out now, Mrs Ashby. One more push." She reddened once more, her fists tightened against the bed sheets, and an infant's cry tore through the room like a blade.

"It's a boy!" cried Hannah, who appeared to be busying herself with some implements I had not previously noticed. Mrs Ashby herself had collapsed upon the bed, and I assisted her to lie on her back. The babe was small, red, and screaming furiously, but nobody seemed concerned at this. Hannah had fussed over it for some time, and then she handed it to Mrs Ashby who took the child to her breast. At that moment, a squat woman in her middle years, flustered and short of breath, burst into the room.

"Oh, Annie, I am sorry to keep you waiting for me. I had trouble with little Clara—oh, good gracious." She fell silent as her eyes fell upon the suckling babe and then moved to me sitting beside its mother.

"Good afternoon, Mrs Cutler, I assume. I am Mrs Darcy. And this is

Miss Taverner. We are pleased to meet you." I looked at Mrs Ashby, and seeing that she was quite beyond speech, I added, "This is the new baby Ashby, who, I am sure, is pleased to meet us all, particularly his mama."

As soon as I heard the beat of hooves upon the ground outside, I knew it was him. To save the ladies the embarrassment that would surely ensue from Mr Darcy's knocking on the door at such a moment, I precipitated him and flew outside just as he was descending from his horse to the muddy ground. An urge to rush to him and fling myself into his arms rose inside me like a wave, but I was still. I was—I realised—wearing neither bonnet nor spencer and had just acted the part of local midwife to a tenant farmer's wife whilst taking orders from my maid. It was not what I imagined he expected from me, and I was suddenly afraid of his reaction. However, it was not anger but confusion that swept over his face. He looked at me hard and moved towards me without hesitation.

"Elizabeth, my God! You have been gone all day. What has kept you here?"

"It is Mrs Ashby's babe. He has been born, Fitzwilliam! Her time was upon her when we arrived, and there was nobody else to help. I could not leave her. I hope I did right."

He looked shocked, and his eyes turned away from me slightly. I explained that Mrs Cutler was now on hand, and all appeared to be well in any case, and so we agreed that Hannah and I should return to Pemberley without further ado. It was late. The light was seeping from the sky, and the air was chillier than before. As it happened, our failure to return home earlier had caused a degree of panic. Mrs Reynolds could not recall which tenants we intended to visit, and although James, one of the footmen, had seen us leave, he had not observed our direction of travel. The result was that servants were sent out in all directions to look for us. My husband, who knew I had been worrying about the Ashbys, thought it most likely I would have visited them, and so he set out himself for their cottage. A band of men was combing the woods on foot behind him, and he commanded them to escort Hannah, who presently appeared with my cloak and bonnet, back to Pemberley.

"We shall ride, Elizabeth," he said turning to me.

"Is somebody bringing Mrs Wollstonecraft?"

"No. You will ride with me." His hands enclosed my waist, and he lifted me atop his great steed as he spoke. The animal was far taller than my gentle horse, and the distance between me and the ground, as well as my anxiety about how two grown people should ride atop the same horse, troubled me.

"Do not fear, Elizabeth," he said as he mounted the horse behind me, his left hand pulling my belly in towards him. He told me to lean back into his body, and I did. It was easy to put myself in his hands, and I did so without hesitation. The ride back to the house was fast and furious. Outside of a carriage, I had never in my life travelled at such speed. The horse's hooves thundered against the damp ground, and chill air lashed my skin as the sky darkened. We went a different route than Hannah and I had taken, and Mr Darcy seemed to know the path by instinct. I felt his strong, hard body behind my back and his breath upon my cheek. He said nothing. When we arrived back at Pemberley, he squeezed me so slightly that I wondered whether it had really happened. As he helped me to the ground, I searched his eyes for some clue, but he gave me none. The light was nearly gone, and I believe he looked away from me. The concerned faces of Georgiana and Mrs Reynolds peered at me as we walked in through the great front door. Was I all right, they wanted to know, and should I like a hot bath? I only nodded and smiled the best smile I could muster. I was suddenly so fatigued and worn by the day's dramas that I could hardly stand and begged to be excused to my rooms.

"I shall take you up." Mr Darcy offered me his arm stiffly.

We ascended the stairs, and every inch we travelled seemed to be a torment. My body was heavy with fatigue, and I was famished. Candlelight flickered against his hard, handsome face.

"You are angry," I said as we arrived in my sitting room.

"I am not angry, Elizabeth... I was worried though. I cannot believe it could not have been... better handled. Mrs Reynolds had *no idea* where you were. I thought you met with her every morning?"

"We do. We did. But this morning, we discussed the Bingley visit. I did not realise I had to report to her!"

"For your own safety, she should know where you are bound. I should have asked you where you were going, and *you* should have told *both* of us. Pemberley is not Longbourn. You cannot wander off whenever the fancy takes you without a word to anyone. This estate is much larger, and if you were to encounter trouble or be hurt... well, it does not bear thinking about." He turned away from me, and I felt most unjustifiably scolded. I thought he had finished, but he continued. "I cannot believe it did not occur to you that...*people*...here...would be worried when you did not return. Why on earth did you not send Hannah back with a message if you could not leave yourself?"

"Because I could not possibly have assisted Mrs Ashby without her. I have never officiated at a child's birth, Fitzwilliam. I *hope* rather than *assume* this does not surprise you." I glanced at his face but saw no evidence he had taken my meaning. "Hannah *has* and knows what she is about. Mrs Ashby was all alone in the cottage with only the children, and she was...well, she was in great straits with her condition. The only alternative would have been for me to walk back to Pemberley through the wood alone, leaving Hannah, and I do not believe you would have approved."

"No, certainly not."

"Well then, I do not believe I had any choice. I did what I thought I must do in the circumstances and...well...maybe it is better to say no more about it." I turned away from him, my head aching, and my body wilting. "I am very tired, sir. If you do not mind, I will go to bed."

His footsteps approached me, and I held my breath. He did not touch me, but I felt him close. I could tell from his tone that he had softened. Had I convinced him? Had he heard my voice and understood me? Did I dare hope he regretted his severity to me before? "Elizabeth, you have not eaten. Did you have luncheon?"

"No. There was no time."

"In that case, you shall certainly not go without your supper as well." His hands clasped my shoulders and sent a shiver through my body. He turned me to him. "If I have a tray of food fetched up here, will you allow me to join you?"

"Yes, of course."

"Good." He released his grip on me and rang the bell. "I shall send a maid for you and join you in half an hour. We shall not stay up late, but you cannot go to bed without food." With that, he removed from the room, and one of the younger maids soon attended me; she righted my hair and helped me out of my muddy frock and into a fresh one. I thought of poor Hannah, trudging through the wood in the cold with strange men for company.

"Do you know whether Hannah has returned yet, Milly?"

"I do not know, madam. I have not seen her. Is she a-walking from Haddon?"

"Yes, she is. When she comes in, please, will you tell her that there is no need to check on me? She should go to bed directly."

"Yes, ma'am," she said quietly as she left the room.

By the time Mr Darcy joined me, I was dozing in a chair by the fire in my sitting room. My eyes blinked open to see him kneeling on the carpet before me and brushing a stray curl from my face. "Elizabeth? Our supper is here." He indicated a tray spread with plenty and a jug of wine. He smiled tenderly. "You should eat something and then retire. You look very pale. I can see it has been a trying day. I am sorry I spoke harshly before."

"Well—"

"I . . . you should know I do not reproach you. I do not think you have done anything wrong. But I think in future, I would like a footman to accompany you and whoever is with you."

He was not asking me whether I agreed; he was telling me it would be so, and I was too tired to argue. The new gentleness in his tone was not lost on me, and as I have said, when I was alone with him, I wanted nothing more than to please him. And so, as on many previous occasions, I smiled, and he smiled, and the matter remained unresolved. We ate our small repast, and after some trifling talk of the estate and the wet weather, during which I was almost too tired to contribute, it was agreed that we should retire. My eyes were barely open as Milly eased me out of my dress and into my nightgown and brushed my hair. She was about to plait it when I interrupted her. "Please, leave it loose, Milly. Thank you. That will be all."

"Yes, madam," she said as she bobbed her way out of the room.

When Mr Darcy arrived, I was just settling myself into the middle of the bed. He caught me arranging my long hair on the pillow, and as he approached, I pushed the cover down for him and smiled. He stroked my arm before climbing into bed beside me. "No, Elizabeth, you are fatigued." He snuffed out the candle and pulled me into his embrace. His scent enveloped my senses, and his voice echoed through my head. All at once—inexorably, unstoppably, blissfully—I fell asleep.

Chapter Nine

I awoke early on the morning Mr Bingley and his sisters were to arrive to find my husband had risen early and was nowhere to be seen. Hannah drew back the great heavy curtains, and light flew across the room, crashing into every corner and making me squint.

"Good morning, madam. Your bath is drawn when you are ready."

"Thank you, Hannah. Do you know where Mr Darcy is?"

"Yes, madam. He is in the library with Mr Franks."

I could not imagine what would take Mr Darcy to meet with his steward at this time of the morning, but I thought no more of it and allowed Hannah to wash and dress me, indulging her when she chose a slightly more decorative dress than I would usually wear for an ordinary day at home. She said nothing, but I understood she did not want me disgraced in front of Miss Bingley and Mrs Hurst. Hannah and I had discussed the Bingley party in veiled terms, and she had revealed that they had often been visitors to Pemberley; Miss Bingley and Mrs Hurst, however, were by no means favoured by the staff. Mr Bingley, she reported, was widely liked below stairs, and it was a pleasure to serve him. I felt it would be disloyal to disparage my husband's guests explicitly, but I think she understood that my view was scarcely different. In any case, I sought to control my anxiety by rarely talking about their visit; it suited me not to recount the attitude the ladies had shown to me in Hertfordshire or that I had not seen any of them since before I married.

Knowing Mr Franks was with my husband, I did not seek him out when I had broken my fast but sat in the music room with Georgiana, singing for her. We had been practicing for some time and were laughing at a wrong note of mine when Mr Darcy appeared. He closed the door behind his back and smiled, but it was immediately apparent that he was discomforted.

"Good morning, Elizabeth. Georgiana."

"Good morning, Fitzwilliam. Are you well?"

"Yes, I am well...I am well. Elizabeth, would you join me in my study, please?"

I was not at all pleased at his imperious tone and perplexed at the cause, but I kissed Georgiana on the head and followed him from the room. "Am I to have a scolding, sir?"

"Certainly not, Elizabeth. Whatever gave you that idea?"

"Well, firstly, I woke alone, and then you summoned me in a most stern manner to your study. I feel quite as though I am about to be censured."

"But you must know you have done nothing wrong."

"Indeed, I have not, but the world is not always a just place, sir." I tilted my head and smiled, but he did not laugh. His expression was more grave than ever. I read concern in his eyes and began to regret my flippancy. "What is wrong, Fitzwilliam? Have you heard from Mr Bingley?"

"No, I have not heard from Bingley. As far as I know, they should be on the road to us now. They always stay at the Inn at Rowsley, so they should be somewhere on the road between there and here. Elizabeth, I do not want you to worry about this unduly, but I am going to ride out to meet them."

"Whatever for? I shall come with you."

"No, no, you will not. You shall stay here with Georgiana, and I would like you both to remain indoors, please. Now, I do not want to make you uneasy, but I have had a report of a robbery by highwaymen on the road from Rowsley. It was last night, but there have been rumours for some days. That is one of the reasons I was so concerned when you did not return yesterday. The truth is that, two days ago, masked men were seen by one of the gamekeepers on the edge of the estate. I did not want to say anything to you last night. There was no point in worrying you, and I was so relieved you were safe. The search party sent out for you did not discover them, and I believed they were gone. However, it seems they are not, and last night, a gang of highwaymen held up and robbed Lady Bellamy's carriage. That is why Franks was here so early this morning. They were last seen making their way north along the Matlock road. So, I am concerned firstly, that they may be on Pemberley land or close by. And secondly, Bingley and his sisters may be riding straight into the path of danger. I have already sent a number of men out to the perimeter, and I will ride out myself with others until we find Bingley and his party and escort them to Pemberley."

His words seemed to slice through me, and I was shocked to the marrow. The nearness of danger and the peril he would be in pounded my head and made my mouth dry. My body felt weak, and I sank onto the chaise. "Oh, Fitzwilliam, it is so dangerous!"

"You are not in danger, Elizabeth. Just stay inside the house."

"I mean dangerous for *you*! You cannot ride out on just your horse when there may be highwaymen! They are most treacherous, and they will be *armed*! They must be very accomplished horsemen."

"I am an accomplished horseman, Elizabeth, and I will have other men with me. I cannot ask others to put themselves in the way of danger and not do so myself. I cannot allow my guests to walk into uncertain catastrophe on the way to our home when it is within my power to stop it. You must see that."

The truth of his words and the inevitability of it, of course, I knew. I suddenly remembered him telling me during our short engagement that he was not a princeling and knew at that moment he spoke true. There was a deeply rooted and unusual bravery within him, one that I would have to accept. "Yes, I do see that. But I am wretched with fear for you. Please do nothing reckless, Fitzwilliam. Shall I say nothing to Georgiana?"

"Yes, that would be best. Thank you." He then kissed me with great tenderness, first on the lips and then on the side of my neck, and was gone.

The rest of the day passed in lonely turmoil as I played the pianoforte, ate luncheon with Georgiana, and mentioned nothing of the great danger her brother faced. I glanced out of the window at the familiar landscape often but saw no sign of any person: friend or foe. I hoped with all my heart that Mr Darcy would appear in the golden light, atop his horse and well. Georgiana, in ignorance of what was occurring or might be occurring, had other concerns.

"Oh, Elizabeth, I am so grateful for this practice if I am to play before Mr Bingley's sisters. They are frightful judges, are they not?"

I smiled to think all of Miss Bingley's attention to Georgiana had only served to intimidate the poor child. "Well, they have very firm notions of accomplishment, Georgiana, but I think you more than come up to scratch as far as they are concerned. I know they admire your playing very much, and I am sure you have nothing to fear. In any case, your brother and I will be here, and I hope we are not frightful judges. Mr Bingley certainly is not."

"No, that is true." She laughed her way through the familiar passage she was playing and seemed to want to say more. "Did you see very much of them when you were in Hertfordshire?"

"Yes, quite a lot. Mr Bingley rented a house only three miles from my home, and I stayed there for three days once when my sister was taken ill during supper with Miss Bingley and Mrs Hurst. Your brother was there, too. They hosted a ball to which the whole neighbourhood was invited..." I was on the verge of saying that Mr Darcy and I had become engaged at the ball, or because of the ball, but my old familiar restraint swelled up inside me, and I stopped myself. Georgiana's sweet face looked at me over the top of the sheet music, and I realised in that moment that I had a desperate desire to talk about Fitzwilliam and the strange unknowns of how we came to be married as well as the mystery of the Bingley party's departure from Netherfield. I had come to love and trust Georgiana, but because I loved her, I could not confide in her. No man was more perfect to her than her brother, and I could not be the one to cast doubts. How could I tell her that I knew not how he felt about me, and he had only married me to avoid a scandal manufactured by my mother?

"Yes, Elizabeth? What about the ball? I am not allowed to attend balls yet."

"Erm, well, it was a ball and it was very merry. After the ball, I became engaged to your brother, but Mr Bingley and his sisters had already departed for town, so I have not seen them since that evening. Mr Bingley is a very agreeable gentleman, and I look forward to renewing my acquaintance with him very much."

"Yes, Charles is very amiable, and I like him, too. You will not persuade me to be easy with Miss Bingley though, Elizabeth."

"Oh yes, I will, for we are sisters now, are we not? I shall protect you from Miss Bingley."

She moved up on the piano bench to make way for me, and I took my place for my side of our duet. "Thank you, Lizzy," she said and kissed my cheek.

I had asked Baxter to tell me immediately when Mr Darcy or anyone else was seen approaching the house. When, in the late afternoon, he appeared in the door of the music room, my heart quaked with fear. "Mrs Darcy, the master and Mr Bingley's carriage have been seen on the road."

"Thank you, Baxter. How far away are they?"

"They were at the milepost, madam."

"I will wait at the door. Thank you."

I fled to the main door, my palms wet with sweat and my mind racing. I hardly noticed Georgiana following me and then standing beside me at the top of the stone steps. Before long he appeared, riding some paces ahead of the carriage and looking exhausted but uninjured. Relief flooded through me like a torrent, and I longed to run to him. I did not do so but stood in the doorway, my heart singing at the sight of him. Safe. Returned. His eyes held mine, and he dismounted without breaking the connection between us. Despite myself, I could be still no longer, and I left our sister's side and flew down the steps towards him. In the seconds that elapsed between Mr Darcy reaching me and the Bingley carriage drawing up, my husband discreetly brushed a kiss on the inside of my wrist.

"All is well, Elizabeth. They had not even left the inn when I arrived, and we have seen nothing untoward. I take it you and Georgiana have nothing to report."

"No, nothing has happened here. You must have been riding for thirty miles."

"Do not think of that…"

We greeted our guests out of their carriage, and they greeted us with carefully rehearsed expressions of joy. The feathers atop Miss Bingley's head bobbed before me, and the swell of Mrs Hurst's extravagant skirts swished about the steps. It was clear from the outset that they had not been told of the danger and were under the impression Mr Darcy had ridden to meet them out of an excess of hospitality.

"How agreeable of you, sir, to ride out to Gravenshurst to meet us. We are so very obliged," cooed Miss Bingley, brushing her hand against my husband's arm. "But then we have always been made to feel so welcome at dear Pemberley, and I can see your marriage has altered nothing! My dear Eliza, how small you look next to Mr Darcy. I do hope you are well. I expect you have been walking a great deal, or have you curtailed your walking now you find yourself in different circumstances?"

"Thank you, Miss Bingley. I am well. And indeed, I have been finding many wonderful walks around Pemberley. I have been riding, too, so I am becoming quite the adventuress."

"How satisfactory for you. I doubt there was much opportunity for riding at Longbourn. You must be quite content with your situation."

"I am, but I have not been denied the opportunity to ride in the past as my father keeps a horse. It is rather I now have an exemplary teacher, who makes all the difference." I shot a glance at Mr Darcy, which Miss Bingley was too quick to miss. Any doubt I had that her behaviour towards me was motivated by jealousy evaporated at that moment, and I found myself pitying her. Objectionable as she was, after the hours of torment I had known, I could not find the space in my mind to be concerned with her.

Our supper passed in ease and enjoyment. We sat in the small dining room, Mr Darcy and I at each end of the table, and I watched the candlelight glowing and flickering across his tired, handsome features. The dishes were served, the drinks were poured, and all were merry. Mr Bingley entertained us with stories of his Scarborough relations and even Mr Hurst, whom I had never seen raise his eyes from his plate before, spoke. Miss Bingley continued to show too much attention to my husband, and although he had never spoken of it to me, I knew it did not signify, and I did not care. Both of Mr Bingley's sisters expressed interest in Pemberley's history, her architecture, and origins. Mr Darcy, who I presumed had taken too much wine, offered to speak of these matters on a tour of the older parts of the house on the morrow, so the ladies were well pleased. Georgiana joined us for supper, and she was thrilled to be allowed to dine with adults outside of her family for the first time. She sat beside me and glanced at me for reassurance, but on the whole, she disported herself admirably. Nobody observing her could have thought anything wanting.

After supper, the ladies played, and I sang while Georgiana accompanied me. Mrs Hurst made sure to compliment Georgiana's playing and not mention my voice, but I had seen my husband looking at me as I sang and could not care for her opinion. While her sister focussed on my sister, Miss Bingley raised a subject that I knew to be unavoidable.

"My dear, Eliza. How very shocked we all were by your marriage! I wonder you ever fancied yourself Mrs Darcy while we were all at Netherfield. It never occurred to me, I must say."

"Well..." I searched for some response but did not find it ready, and she continued.

"And for it to have taken place too quickly! I cannot imagine what must have prompted such speedy nuptials... No sooner had we arrived in town than our brother received word our dear, new acquaintance, Eliza Bennet, was Mrs Darcy, without a word to anyone or even our brother being in attendance."

"Erm, well—"

"And your poor mother! Surely, Mrs Bennet cannot have been satisfied with a hasty wedding. She would have wanted to invite all of her four and twenty families; I am sure. However did you persuade her, Mr Darcy, to part with her daughter with such alacrity? What say you, sir? You must be quite the romantic to carry Eliza off in so little time?"

Mr Darcy did not suffer my uncertainty in his reply. "Our wedding was a quiet affair, Miss Bingley. I hope our friends can forgive us that. As to being a romantic, I cannot say. I am not given to publishing my private affairs and do not intend to start now. But suffice to say, I am not a man to delay matters of importance."

Her enquiry unanswered, Miss Bingley seemed to know the subject was closed. Mr Darcy had flicked the slightest glance at me as he spoke these words. What was his meaning? Did he look away because he was unhappy or because he did not wish to be observed? Whatever the truth, I had the solace that my husband would not tolerate further discussion of the matter and resolved to be as cheerful as possible with our guests. Thus, the remainder of the evening passed in agreeable discussion, the tinkling of Miss Bingley's laugh following Mr Darcy's every remark. At length, well fed and entertained, our guests retired; having briefly checked with Mrs Reynolds that the arrangements for the morrow were in place, I did likewise.

I was sitting up in bed with my book when Mr Darcy arrived in the doorway between our chambers. To see his face, exhausted and slightly shadowed, moved me greatly. The relief I had felt upon seeing him approaching the house and the hours of worry I had known that day returned to me in an instant, and I crawled towards him across the bed. Without pausing, he met me and, leaning against the foot of my bed, embraced me. Something unknown seemed to have shifted, and when he kissed me, he kissed not just my face, but my neck, my bosom, my belly. A fury was within him. His touch was strong, but I did not fear him. Raising his head from my chest, he gestured to my nightgown. "May I remove this, Elizabeth?"

Shocked as I was, I consented, and he pulled the garment over my head and cast it upon the floor in one motion. He had never, in all our marriage, seen my nakedness but to my great surprise, I did not feel shy. The pleasure of his attentions was a source of amazement to me, and I could not speak. No words were necessary, however, for we seemed to understand one another well enough. My husband gently pushed me back and, atop the blanket, our bodies uncovered, made love to me with such urgency that I knew he had hungered for it. The pleasure of it spilled through my body like a flood, and I was drowned. When it was over, I trembled in his arms.

"Forgive me; I am a brute to make you cold," he said as he tucked me beneath the rumpled blankets.

"I am not cold, and there is nothing to forgive. I was going to ask you about your journey and the highwaymen, Fitzwilliam, but now I feel I cannot focus on sensible conversation."

He laughed. "I am pleased to hear that I can *distract* you so, Elizabeth. I...well...I had feared I could not."

I rolled atop him, emboldened by my happiness and said, "You can," before we kissed more.

LATER, WE DID CONVERSE ON the events of the day.

"Fitzwilliam, you should sleep now. You must be exhausted, and you have promised Miss Bingley and Mrs Hurst a narrative history of Pemberley in the morning."

"Yes, that was a rash promise. Maybe I should ask Georgiana to deliver it, I have never seen her so confident in front of Bingley's sisters. Anyway, I thought you wanted to know about the highwaymen. I am afraid they have not been apprehended. We saw nothing of them or their like on the road in either direction, and no one on the estate has seen them. Lord Bellamy's messenger came this evening to say they do not have them and do not know their whereabouts. I am worried they may hide in our woods, Elizabeth, so you will have to stay indoors again tomorrow. I am sorry. I know you will miss your walks, especially with our guests here."

"Is it possible to search the woods?"

"Yes, and it was partly done today. The men will continue tomorrow, and I will join them for a few hours."

He felt me flinch at his words and locked me still tighter in his arms, kissing my head until I fell into slumber. As I lay in his embrace, I had never felt closer to him. The warmth of his physical affection was some replacement for his lack of words to me and the anxiety I felt about the basis of our marriage. Our bodies had met and conversed in the same language. If I could have nothing else with him, then I had that. Should I not be grateful for the blessings God gives me? With that, my mind turned to my condition, to the small life within me, rising like bread in a hot oven, waiting for no man. I knew I must face it, and in this new intimacy with Fitzwilliam, I felt ready to tell him I was with his child. I resolved to do so as soon as the Bingley party had departed.

Chapter Ten

The days in which Mr Bingley and his family were our guests passed quite reasonably. On the second day of their stay, a message reached us that the highwaymen had been spotted on the road to Glossop and were believed gone out of the country. From that time on, we entertained our guests out of doors as well as within. In fine weather, unchallenging walks were undertaken, and the men rode before breakfast. Inevitably, the ladies were forced to spend many hours together, and though none of us would have chosen this, nothing untoward occurred. Miss Bingley and Mrs Hurst were clearly perplexed at my marriage and ignorant of the circumstances. However much they may have wished to pry, they could not risk doing so in front of Georgiana, so they said nothing on the subject.

Neither did they say very much about my family. I suspected them of wishing to avoid the subject of my sister Jane lest their brother be reminded of her beauty and goodness and wish to return to Netherfield. I had formed the opinion that they had been the force separating my sister from Mr Bingley. Therefore, they contented themselves with merely referring *in general terms* to my lack of accomplishment and society. In passing, they commented repeatedly on my unfamiliarity with town and inexperience in managing large houses. Each gown I wore was remarked as being an improvement on the simple muslins I had been accustomed to in Hertfordshire. Even my diminutive size was taken to be a sign of inadequacy, although I knew I was growing fat, and my breasts were swollen and sore.

Between my husband and me, the subsequent nights passed in much the same manner as the first. My feelings for him, long in their formation, had taken flight. Some silent inhibition between us had come away, and in the privacy of our quarters, we became free with one another. In his public attitude towards me, there was not one indication, but in private, we had ignited. Still, he said very little and did not allay my fears with respect to his general attitude towards my family and background. He did give me confidence; however, in the privacy of my bedchamber and between our unclothed bodies, he was not indifferent to me.

On his last night at Pemberley, Mr Bingley was presented with his favourite dish at supper, and I think he was well pleased. He smiled like a child at Christmas and was as gracious as he was jolly. During our pudding course, he eyed me nervously and, stammering, asked me whether *all* of my sisters were still at Longbourn.

Knowing instantly that he asked of Jane, I tested his feelings. "Not *all*, Mr Bingley..." I allowed the potential of my words to sit on the air before continuing. "My next sister, Mary, is lately married and now resides in Kent. I, of course, am here. Otherwise, we are all as we were before."

Relief suffused his face, and after a short and uncharacteristic silence, he began to reminisce. "You know, Mrs Darcy, I can hardly remember a happier time than those short months I spent at Netherfield. What a merry party we were at the ball. I can scarcely remember such a joyous evening. I must say that I did find the society in Hertfordshire quite splendid."

"Well, sir, I believe you were much missed when you departed. My mama, in particular, has not forgotten you are owed a family supper at Longbourn. And I am sure it would be a great scandal if you did not indulge her!"

He beamed his ready smile, and his eyes brightened with the merriment that was his wont. "I think you must be right, Mrs Darcy. I would not have Mrs Bennet offended, so maybe I should arrange to visit Netherfield again soon. Are you certain?" And here he seemed to linger over his words. I looked at him steadily, willing him to continue. "Are you certain, Mrs Darcy, I should be welcomed?"

"Quite certain, sir," said I without hesitation and with a small smile I hoped was encouraging. My spirits were lifted by the thought that he may be guided back to Jane.

Later, when the ladies retired to the drawing room, I wondered whether my conversation with Mr Bingley had been overheard by his sister. I had tried to keep my voice low, but Caroline Bingley is not a woman to be unobservant. She began to dwell on Mary's marriage, and all attended to it. "Remind me of your next sister's name, Eliza? I must confess I could never quite commit all of the Bennet girls to memory."

"My sister Mary, Miss Bingley. She is now Mrs Collins."

"Yes, of course—Miss Mary Bennet, who as I recall was quite the musician. Who could forget her performances? I imagine the society in Kent is feeling quite spoiled! What says Mr Darcy? Shall he be tempted to send Georgiana to practise with the new Mrs Collins?" Georgiana, ignorant of my sister's shortcomings as a pianist, was confused but cognisant enough of Miss Bingley's tone to be embarrassed. She blushed and looked at her lap. "And what of your new brother, Eliza? Does he have an estate?"

"He is a clergyman, Miss Bingley. I assume you would not disapprove. As to an estate—well, Longbourn is entailed upon him."

"No, indeed. I am sure your sister has done very well and made a very respectable match. Not *all* of your sisters, after all, could expect your good fortune. As I have said before, we were quite astounded, Eliza, to hear in December that you were Mrs Darcy. We had had no notion such a thing might occur. Of course, you have done very well, my dear, and I am sure your mother is thrilled, but we were all staggered. It was such an odd business. After all, it was *dear* Mr Darcy who encouraged us all to leave for town after the ball." She spoke these last words slowly and carefully as if there was some danger of my failing to understand their meaning. "I particularly recall... the very next morning, my brother was called to town on a matter of business, and Louisa and I were only too pleased to leave for some respite from the country. But it was *Darcy* who said Charles had no reason to return, and there was *no particular person or persons* to keep him at Netherfield as compared to the pleasures of town. He was so certain of that. How odd he should have stayed himself and married you so swiftly."

She let the silence settle around her words. Her skirts rustled around her as she walked about the room. "Of course, you shall be in town yourself soon, no doubt, and Mr Darcy's townhouse is so graceful and convenient for the theatre. Remind me where your London family live, Eliza? Yes, of course, I recall your sister telling us: Cheapside. Well, I am sure you will find your new home in town vastly more convenient, so convenient that you may find it a challenge to visit your aunt and uncle at such a distance."

I knew she would never have gone so far had Mr Darcy been present.

The knowledge of her spite and jealousy sat in my mind like a stone, but it availed me little. Although I knew she spoke with malice, I was also certain she spoke the truth. I recalled the strange speed of my entanglement with Mr Darcy and the departure of the Netherfield party. It was obvious to anyone who cared to look that Mr Bingley deferred to his friend's judgement. My mind reeled to remember the times my husband had avoided the subject, pleaded ignorance, and redirected my anxiety about Jane. I realised in that moment that he had been even more contemptuous of my family than I had thought. How he must despise us! How little he must care for our feelings if he could act so towards my sister. I blushed at the thought of how completely I had given myself to him these past nights. It can have meant nothing to him beyond passing physical pleasure, and I was mortified at his opinion of me now. I thought, too, of all the things I did not know: Mr Darcy's reasons for marrying me so readily, his separating my sister from Mr Bingley, the mysterious house in Queen Anne's Gate, and Mrs Woodham and her fluttering hands. They crowded in on me all at once.

When the men joined us, I had schooled my face to conceal my torment. I discussed Napoleon with Mrs Hurst and played a duet with Georgiana. I forced myself to meet Miss Bingley's eye but only to prove to myself that I could. Mr Darcy, I believed, noticed no change in me and appeared as he always did. When our guests had retired, we retired ourselves, and I willed myself to be as he expected. However, my heart was broken, and my soul was wretched. The fragile and incomplete thing between us had splintered, and I knew not how it should ever be repaired.

Chapter Eleven

As we journeyed to Rosings Park, my thoughts were of my unborn child. He or she had almost become a character in my life. My breasts were heavy and tender, and slight green veins snaked around their fullness. Under my skirts and so slightly it was known only to me, my belly was swelling. More than this, I felt different. When Hannah left me in my bath or I walked in the walled garden before supper, I no longer felt alone. And yet, I knew that, were he to be aware of my condition, Mr Darcy would care for me as any husband should. However, since Miss Bingley's awful revelation, I could not tell him. His betrayal of me and his wounding of my sister, I found cruel to bear. I felt quite crushed under the responsibility of carrying his child in such circumstances.

Our carriage would sprint through the countryside for three days to reach Kent. Mr Darcy sat beside me whilst I dozed on his shoulder. We had travelled the rough terrain of the Pennine Hills, and now the more subdued, rolling country around Hertfordshire opened before us. We did have some conversation, for even Mr Darcy could not be confined with another person in a carriage for three days without speaking a little. As we rolled into the gentle countryside of my home shire, I braved a subject rarely mentioned between us.

"How close to Longbourn we must be."

"Actually, it is some distance. Meryton is 10 miles from the main road, and parts of the journey are poor. You would be surprised how long it would take us to reach it from here."

Frustration grew in me, and I wanted to say that, were *his* parents and siblings a mere ten miles hence, bad roads would not keep us from them. The familiar caution of my married life took over, and I did not share my thoughts. "I wonder when I shall see my family again, Fitzwilliam. Seeing Hertfordshire makes me quite nostalgic for them."

"You shall see Mrs Collins at Rosings, Elizabeth. You will have plenty of time with her in these two weeks, and in any case, surely Georgiana and I are your family now." He spoke quickly, and his clipped tone told me he was growing irritated. I also was irritated, and the injustice of his words burned.

"Yes, of course," I said, incensed for not speaking out more and wanting to stoke his anger as I had when we first met. Beside him, I simmered, staring out the carriage window at the passing fields and villages. Silence hung between us for some time, and as usual, it was I who was forced to break it. "Tell me about Lady Catherine?"

He smiled one of his half smiles and drew me close to him. "Lady Catherine is my mother's younger sister. Her husband—my uncle—died some years ago, and so it is just she and my cousin Anne at Rosings. Anne is just a few months my junior, but she has always had poor health, unfortunately. She and Lady Catherine rarely leave Rosings, but I believe my aunt encourages plenty of visits by way of society. I suspect we will see a lot of Mr Collins, for example. Lady Catherine is usually very attentive to the rector of the church at Hunsford."

"I wonder his manner would not put her off."

"No, I very much doubt that, Elizabeth. My aunt... well, she cannot have too much praise."

He smiled, and I wondered what he was keeping back. I recalled the endless prattling of Mr Collins and thought, not for the first time, that the famous Lady Catherine must be a singular sort of woman.

"And what of your cousin, sir? Are you close?"

"Anne? No, not at all. We are the same age, but she has always been so sickly, she remains within doors most of the time. Since my father's death, I have spent Easter at Rosings every year, but I have always had Fitzwilliam with me, and we spend much of our time out riding or visiting tenants for Lady Catherine. So, Anne has never really been a part of it. In any case, she says so little. She is quite timid."

"That must be a family trait," I said.

"Georgiana is only shy with those she does not know."

"I did not mean Georgiana." He looked completely perplexed. "I thought of you! *You* say very little." I could not help but laugh.

A wounded look stole over his face, and I realised he thought I was making sport of him. I had not meant to criticise but could not regret having spoken the truth.

"I hope I do not waste time saying things which do not need saying, Elizabeth. If you have been missing conversation, then you will find plenty at Rosings. I daresay, between my aunt and your cousin, you will be quite overwhelmed."

"I did not mean to criticise, Fitzwilliam, but...well...I worry you do not speak to me more because it is not agreeable for you to do so."

"I do not have the pleasure of understanding you, Elizabeth. Of course, it is agreeable to speak to you. In any case, with Anne it is completely different. She does not speak because she does not have the confidence to do so. It is very hard to get anything at all out of her." With that, he kissed my hair and closed the subject.

Our arrival at Rosings, delayed as we were by poor weather, was in the early evening. Hannah had dressed me in one of my better day gowns of pale green silk, and I had never alighted anywhere in such finery. My husband had said nothing of my appearance, but he had held me for many miles. It was a blow to my comfort when, as we reached the perimeter of Rosings Park, he withdrew his arm and straightened, staring out of the carriage window and away from me.

The entrance hall, where we were received, was a most ornate room, and in the half-light, I could scarcely take it in. Rich canvasses and whitened sculptures seemed to unfold on all sides and enclose us. When the mistress of the house appeared, my eyes could hardly account for her. Lady Catherine stood several inches taller than me and, although it was not hot, waved a silk fan before her lined face. Her skirts were so thick that I fancied they looked like curtains.

"Darcy! Is that my nephew? Where have you been? We expected you hours ago! It is most vexing when visitors are late, and I cannot abide it."

"I am sorry, Lady Catherine; we were delayed by rain. Lady Catherine, may I present my wife, Mrs Darcy."

She turned her large grey eyes on me for the first time. "Yes, I imagined you must be Mrs Darcy." She seemed to look me up and down and scarcely looked pleased when she said, "Welcome."

I curtseyed to her and raised my eyes to see she had turned away and was addressing my husband. "Fitzwilliam is already here; *he* was not delayed at all, and he *rode* from town. Now I shall leave you and see you at supper. I trust that you will not delay that as well."

Astonished as I was at this reception, I determined to say nothing. Having easily established good relations with Lord and Lady Matlock, as well as Colonel Fitzwilliam and Georgiana, I expected there was hope for Lady Catherine and me. Hannah and Mr Darcy's valet immediately went below stairs, and a footman and housemaid from Rosings showed us to our chambers. My husband kissed me lightly on the forehead when they left us, but he said nothing, and we each prepared for supper in our own chambers.

That supper was excessively odd; but for the presence of Colonel Fitzwilliam, it would have been entirely wretched. Since we had been married less than a year, I was seated next to my husband whose conversation, scarce as it was, was directed at everyone but me. Miss Anne de Bourgh said not an audible word throughout the meal, only occasionally nodding in the direction of her mother or cousins when they spoke. Lady Catherine, as it transpired, spoke enough for all her family and seldom required a response. Her attitude to me was no less strident than it was entrenched.

"You do not appear to have an appetite, Mrs Darcy. Your sister, Mrs Collins, has an excellent appetite. I hope you are not ill. I have always considered visiting people whilst one is unwell to be most discourteous."

"Indeed ma'am, but I am not ill. I assure you."

"Hmm, well, good." She eyed me with suspicion and turned to Colonel Fitzwilliam. "Mrs Darcy's sister is my parson's wife, Fitzwilliam. You shall meet them both tomorrow. Mrs Collins appears to be a sensible, respectable sort of woman—not brought up too high."

Grateful was I for Colonel Fitzwilliam's manners and kindness when he pointedly turned to me with his reply. "I have already met Mrs Collins, Aunt, at Darcy's wedding. She is a very pleasant lady, and I very much look forward to renewing my acquaintance with her. I am also most anxious to know my new cousin better." He nodded towards me, smiled, and with his eyes seemed to say, *Relax.* "Indeed, I do not recall an Easter when we had so many ladies present, and it is set to be most diverting. What say you, Darcy?"

Mr Darcy appeared completely shocked by his cousin's involving him in this exchange and simply replied, "I do not doubt it, Fitzwilliam," with rather more sternness than I thought was merited.

"Neither do I, Darcy. Mrs Darcy, are you still fond of walking? There are some wonderful walks hereabout in the park. The grove is particularly beautiful at this time of year, and I hope you will enjoy it."

"You may be certain of it, Colonel Fitzwilliam. I could not see the grounds properly when we arrived as we were losing the light, but what I could see looked most promising. I have my hopes fixed on explorations during our stay."

"Do you walk out of doors often then, Mrs Darcy? I have not noticed this trait in Mrs Collins. She, I must say, very sensibly remains indoors attending to her household much of the time."

"I very much enjoy a walk, Lady Catherine. I do not know whether I can tempt my sister to join me though; she has always been a great one for indoor pursuits."

"As well she might be. I am not at all sure it is appropriate for young women to walk extensively. It is far too tiring, and there is nothing in the park that cannot be seen from your carriage. I wonder at your being so different from your sister, Mrs Darcy. You are one of five daughters, are you not? Are you all at such variance from one another?"

"We are quite different, ma'am... but I have often observed that children of the same home often are so. And indeed, I believe it should be encouraged since variety is, as they say, the spice of life, is it not?"

The look of astonishment on my hostess's face was complete, and her eyes flitted between my husband and me. After some time, she replied. "You state your opinions very decidedly for so young a person, Mrs Darcy. Pray, what is your age?"

"I am a married woman with three younger sisters grown up; your ladyship can hardly expect me to own it."

"Come now, Mrs Darcy, I will wager you are younger than my nephew. You cannot be more than one and twenty?"

"I am not yet one and twenty, ma'am," I said, feeling excessively young and under siege.

The time of the evening in which the ladies retired without the men to the drawing room was by far the worst. Lady Catherine, Anne, and I sat around the ornate room like tiny pegs in a sea of brocade. Anne said not a word, nor did she meet my eye, try though I did to catch hers. Lady Catherine spoke on the subject of her garden, the season, her dislike of town, and other subjects too obscure to number. She looked at me in an odd, sideways manner, and each time I bade to speak, she appeared alarmed. When we retired to bed, I was exhausted with the effort of remaining polite and defending myself. Hannah removed my gown, dressed me for bed, and I collapsed, not waiting for Mr Darcy before I fell into a deep slumber.

I awoke in the morning to find him gone. It was clear from the sheets and pillow next to me that he had slept beside me, but I recalled nothing of his coming to bed. I still wore my nightgown and knew he had not loved me in the night. A fear stole over me that I had angered him in some way in the carriage or over supper. I did not want to lose the physical connection between us. We had, it seemed, little enough on which to base a marriage as it was. Thus worried and downcast, I rose and allowed Hannah to dress me as she chose after my bath. When I appeared at breakfast, my husband was at the table and rose to seat me.

"Elizabeth, Fitzwilliam is determined that your walking tours of Rosings are to begin this morning, so we thought we would begin by walking to the parsonage directly after you have broken your fast. Is that agreeable to you?"

"It is; thank you. But do you not wish to ride? I do not wish to keep you from your usual routines."

"You are my wife, Elizabeth. Who else but you should keep me from my usual routines? In any case, I cannot allow Fitzwilliam to monopolise you entirely."

"Well, in that case, it is settled. I am sure we shall be a happy party, sir." He did not laugh at my joke.

So it was that, in the mid-morning sunshine, my husband, Colonel Fitzwilliam, and I walked in harmony to Hunsford. Mr Darcy said little but appeared content and offered me his arm for the journey. Colonel Fitzwilliam was jovial company and entertained us both with tales of his travels and duties. I confessed to finding it most confusing that the colonel's surname was the same as Mr Darcy's first name. It was explained to me, by the colonel, of course, that it was a tradition in the family to give the eldest son his mother's maiden name as a Christian name. I thought of my own child, certain that Mr Darcy would not countenance this tradition if it is a boy, and I was momentarily overcome with sadness. It was resolved, however, that to make matters simpler, I should address Colonel Fitzwilliam as "Richard" and he address me as "…'Elizabeth' or 'Lizzy' if you prefer, sir. All of my family call me 'Lizzy' as does Georgiana." Mr Darcy looked most displeased at this last remark, and I could not begin to understand why.

Our welcome at the parsonage was a profuse one. We spied Mr Collins as we approached, standing at his gate, and he lost no time in gathering Mary from the house and walking out on the path to meet us. My sister I was quite overcome to see. I had never been close to Mary and, in all my months at Pemberley, had longed to see Jane. However, in the moment that I saw Mary's light and pleasing figure heading towards me, an unfamiliar lace cap upon her head, I could barely contain my joy. She smiled, and in her smile, I saw my home, my family, and all that I knew. It was Mr Collins who commenced the pleasantries.

"Mr Darcy! Colonel Fitzwilliam! You honour us with your presence, and we are most delighted to welcome you to our home. Mrs Darcy! My dear cousin! My dear sister, you are most welcome. I little thought when we met in Hertfordshire that I should be welcoming you to my home in these circumstances, but welcome you are! Indeed you are!"

And so the visit progressed with any person other than Mr Collins speaking little and rarely. Unfortunately, my new brother's highest and most lengthy praise was reserved for the person who least wished to receive it: my husband. "It is such an honour to be able to serve my esteemed patroness, but I never thought to be connected to her honoured family by the ties of marriage. Indeed, I did not! What an honour it is, Mr Darcy, to call you 'brother'; indeed, it seems so august I can hardly credit it is true. Not that my dear Mrs Collins and I would ever expect to see Pemberley, but we are told it is quite magnificent and equals even Rosings in style and splendour!"

I felt myself redden with mortification and could scarcely look at Fitzwilliam. I pondered whether he was more affronted at having his relationship to Mr Collins made so explicit or at having his beloved Pemberley compared to the excessive ornamentation of Rosings. The babble of my cousin's eulogising and the clatter of teacups on saucers continued longer than the others present really wished. By the time we departed the Parsonage for the walk back to Rosings, I could feel my husband's dissatisfaction reverberating between us. He spoke not, nor did he offer me his arm. His long legs stalked away, racing down the hill we had climbed in harmony only an hour before. Colonel Fitzwilliam seemed to see his displeasure but did not credit it with sympathy.

"Darcy! Would you make runners of Lizzy and me? Your poor wife will take a fall if we are forced to keep this pace. Slow down, man!"

I saw him stiffen and battle the anger within. He slowed and turned, his handsome face cast against the lush green of the valley. "*Elizabeth*, forgive me. I forget myself." He offered his arm, which I took. He did not look at his cousin as he continued. "As a matter of fact, Fitzwilliam, my wife is an excellent walker, and I am quite sure she could cope with any pace. I would not want to tire *you* though."

"There is not a tired bone in my body, Darcy, as you well know. I could keep going all day. We should plan further walks to show Lizzy the valley and the estate as it stretches towards Westerham. There is a flower meadow I am sure she would love, to say nothing of the view from Ide Hill. What say you?"

"I say they sound excellent prospects, Fitzwilliam, but I will allow Elizabeth to decide. Maybe after some rest."

I well took his meaning and said nothing. There hung in the air a strange tension between the cousins. A rivalry and understanding, from which I was excluded, knitted them together, and I could make no sense of it. I knew my husband was annoyed beyond reckoning, and I ought to placate him. Despite this, I was also wounded that he thought nothing of my own feelings. A rebellious spirit welled up inside me, and I scarce knew how I should stop its growth. Colonel Fitzwilliam seemed able to speak to Mr Darcy as I had seen no other person do, and yet he also had irritated my husband.

That night, I was awake when he joined me in my chamber. He removed his nightshirt wearily and crawled like a tired animal into bed beside me.

"Fitzwilliam, are you well?"

He paused, seeming to search for words. After a moment and with a sigh, he assented. "Yes, I am well." He turned on to his front and locked his eyes with mine. "Shall you need me on your visit to the parsonage tomorrow?"

"No. I know you do not wish to visit there. Actually, Mary and I intend to walk out and, I hope, have some conversation to ourselves. I made a secret pact with her, and I think she will be glad of it."

"Good, well, I hope you enjoy your time with her."

"What about our walks with Richard? Do you wish it?"

"Must the two of you keep to this 'Richard' and 'Lizzy' arrangement? I cannot grow used to it."

"I can return to calling him 'Colonel Fitzwilliam' if you like, but the problem is that you are 'Fitzwilliam' to me. You should have pity on my poor brain."

"Your brain is more than capable of dealing with it, Elizabeth. In any case, I can take you on walks around the estate."

"As you wish. Shall you tell me when?"

"Yes." The silence stuck between us like layered paint.

"Fitzwilliam, is anything else wrong?"

"No," he said turning to me, a familiar look about his face. He kissed me long. "No, there is nothing wrong."

Chapter Twelve

My walks with Mary were strangely peaceful affairs. Mr Collins was busy with his garden and attending Lady Catherine, so he did not have time to join us. Though we had not been together in many months, Mary had lost none of her absurdity, and her remarks were frequently mirthless and gauche. Still, something in her reminded me of Longbourn, and seeing her before me and hearing her soft voice seemed to prove Longbourn and those within still existed. I missed our family desperately whilst I was with her.

"Married life suits me well, Lizzy. I hope it does you. But yes, it suits me very well. Our cousin is a good husband, and I have my own household here. I have no Kitty and Lydia to contend with and no Mama to keep company. There is no talk of balls and assemblies. It is just me and Mr Collins at home, and I find that perfectly agreeable. I do not miss the hubbub of Longbourn."

"I think I do, but I am glad to hear you are happy. Our cousin sounds to be a good husband to you."

"Yes, he is. Now you and I both know about . . . well, what goes on between a husband and his wife. I suppose we can speak of it between ourselves. Well, Lizzy, I am perfectly content. I find the business itself is not as bad as Mama said it would be, and in any case, it is only once a week."

I had not expected such a confidence and did not quite know what to do with it. I was immediately certain I would not confide the truth of Mr Darcy's nightly lovemaking in return. It seemed too precious to share in that way, and I was afraid of reducing its power by discussing it. "Well . . . *good*. I am pleased to hear it. Do you hear from Longbourn?"

"Yes, quite often. Mama writes and Jane also. I have had one letter from Kitty. Everything sounds much the same as ever except you are not there, and nothing is known of Mr Bingley. I am sure you know about that. Mama and Jane are both anxious to hear how your stay here progresses. They... well... they ask me to report that you are *well*—with Mr Darcy, I mean. I hope I can do so?"

I was taken aback by this. I had written to everyone who had written to me and hoped I left no room for doubt of my contentment. What was the use of my situation if, in addition to my worries, my family were also anxious about me?

"Yes... of course. I am very happy with my circumstances. Mr Darcy is... He is a good husband to me, too."

"Good. He seems to say so little and... well, Lizzy... he is awfully stern. It is hard to imagine him within his own quarters. But if you report you are happy, then it must be so. I am sure Mama and Jane will be content."

As promised, my husband escorted me on walks around the estate although Colonel Fitzwilliam accompanied us on a couple of occasions. On Maundy Thursday, the weather was very fine, and the gentlemen agreed I should see the meadow as it stretches towards Brasted. I was to meet them in the music room, and we would set off from the back of the house. Hannah dressed me in my favourite walking gown, and I almost ran to our meeting place. As I approached the music room, I saw the door was slightly ajar. From within I could hear my husband and his cousin, their voices not exactly raised in argument but also not in harmony. Colonel Fitzwilliam used a tone with Mr Darcy I had never heard before.

"Darcy, the whole of London knows of Mrs Lovelace and her 'establishment.' I really do not see that it signifies now. There is too much done. And the fact of the matter is that she will find out at some point—"

"But not at this point, Fitzwilliam. It is far too soon, and I will not have it. No, I shall deal with this issue alone. I will be seeing Mrs Lovelace in town and... well, I will arrange things."

"And what about Mrs Darcy?"

"Mrs Darcy does not need to know."

How I hated those words, and how I hated the feelings of confusion and tumult that beset me. I loathed listening at doors, but then to discover I am a problem to my husband and am to be kept in ignorance of some great secret was too much. It occurred to me to return to our chamber and feign illness, but I suspected he would simply visit me, and I would be forced to face him in even less desirable circumstances. No, it would not do. I straightened my back against the wall outside the music room, filled my lungs, pinched my cheeks, and entered the room.

Had my mind not been on fire with speculation as to the identity of "Mrs Lovelace" and her connection to my husband, I would have enjoyed our walk very much. The way through the woods was cool, clear, and beautiful, and the meadow was speckled with wildflowers of all colours. The air was heavy with the scent of them, and the sun shone upon our heads. When I felt Fitzwilliam's hand upon the small of my back, I could have cried, and if his cousin had not been with us, I probably would have done so. As it was, I forced myself to smile and prayed most ardently for some resolution to my problems.

If there was an aspect of Lady Catherine's patronage that Mr Collins enjoyed even more than being her guest, it was being her spiritual guide. This we were all made aware of during our Easter services. Solemn though Good Friday must necessarily be, my cousin did not neglect to compliment the clothing of Lady Catherine and her daughter as our party arrived at church. He flapped and flustered us to the de Bourgh family pew as though he were conducting the Prince Regent to his seat at the theatre, and I knew Mr Darcy was horrified. Matters were little improved on Easter Sunday when his sermon's principal concern was the distinctions of rank within the Kent community. Lady Catherine's head nodded gently in approval, and I sat between my husband and his cousin—one, incandescent and the other, I suspected, stifling the occasional laugh. Then Mr Collins and Mary joined us for luncheon at Rosings on Easter Sunday.

"Mrs Darcy, you are very glum today. But of course you are; you shall be going away very soon. I am sure you are unused to splendour in houses as you must find at Rosings." I hardly knew what to say to this, and as it turned out, Lady Catherine required little by way of reply. "I understand your father's estate is very small and entailed upon Mr Collins. That must be very disagreeable to grow up away from the advantages of the best society and to contend with an entail as well." She paused for a moment, skewering me with her eyes and raising her chin to continue. "Of course, Pemberley is a fine estate, but you must be quite lost there. A country girl such as you has never been mistress of Pemberley before and...well, I imagine you are quite undone by the expectations."

Mr Darcy interrupted. "Aunt, Elizabeth is a fine mistress and—"

"Yes, yes, but my sister was the last mistress there, and our father was an earl. We grew up on a great estate and have always known their ways. The current Mrs Darcy is at quite a disadvantage, Darcy; you must say that."

"I do not say that, Lady Catherine, and let that be an end to the matter." Then, Mr Darcy moved to the window and turned his back on the room, his rigid fingers clasped behind his back.

Once again, the colonel came to my rescue. "Mrs Darcy, might we impose upon you to play? I am in great need of a song. I hope Mr Collins will not consider me a heathen!"

"Your concern does you credit, Colonel Fitzwilliam, but no, certainly not! Indeed, I do not. I consider music, in the right setting and amongst people of morals, is a great balm to the spirit."

I stood and, before Mr Collins could explain himself further, sat at the instrument and began to play. My playing made me deaf to the conversation in the room, and I was glad. My fingers hammered the keys, and my body was alive with the energy of music. Sound rose from the strings and made an agreeable barrier between my company and me. My husband appeared beside me, bearing gifts of more sheet music. He had selected a number of pieces from Lady Catherine's collection, and I played them all, wordlessly agreeing with him that I was more welcome as a bringer of song than as a relation.

OUR FINAL NIGHT AT ROSINGS was a week after Easter. I had walked the length and breadth of the estate, played after every supper, and tried my best with Fitzwilliam's aunt for over two weeks. I was ready to depart. After dinner, when the ladies retired to the splendours of the drawing room, leaving the men to their whiskey, it was a comfort to know that it was the last time. Steady to my husband's description, Anne said almost nothing throughout our stay, but Lady Catherine never stopped.

"Well, Mrs Darcy, I am sure you already look forward to your visit to Rosings next year. It is quite a tradition, and Darcy is always so sorry to leave, but I suppose he has business in town."

"Yes, ma'am. We are to town for three weeks before returning to Pemberley for the summer, and we shall carry very fond memories of our time here."

"Of course, you cannot have spent very much time in town before, Mrs Darcy. It will be quite new to you, I imagine. You will be most impressed, I am sure. For my part, I was never one for always being in town and going here and there. I have always been most at ease here at Rosings, and so was my late husband. *He* was not the sort of man who needed to visit town as other men do."

"Well..." I was not sure what she suggested, but I suspected it was not intended to comfort me. "I am a country dweller myself, Lady Catherine, so I can sympathise. Your home is very grand, and if you never wish to leave it, then I can well understand."

"Well, then we are as one, Mrs Darcy, which pleases me. I hope you find the married state an agreeable one. You have done very well by your marriage, but I expect you know that." She paused, fingering the blue lace of her sleeve and then, looking up at me, continued. "You may not realise that, when he married you, Darcy broke his engagement to poor Anne." Her great grey eyes stared me down and then, after a beat, glanced gently to her daughter sitting beside her. "Or maybe you did know about it. He may have told you, or he may not have. It is, I suppose, in the past now. He has *begged* my forgiveness, and I have granted it. Darcy knows I could have made more fuss than I did, and I would have been within my rights to do so. It is not the sort of thing he would like people to know: that he broke a promise to a respectable and high-born relation in order to marry a young woman who...well, in order to marry another."

I blinked and felt a lurch within me as though I had fallen from a great height. I recalled Mr Darcy had said little of Anne, even when I asked, and he seemed to grow rather testy when required to discuss her.

"We have resolved not to think on it though, he and I, and I suppose in time it shall be forgotten. I understand from my servants that my nephew keeps to your bedchamber at night. Well, it is early in your marriage, and he has not yet been to town, has he? No, of course, you have been at Pemberley."

My mind reeled at this new direction in her conversation. I was astonished that she had raised such a subject and still more that she should do so with her unmarried daughter sitting beside her. Anne looked away, and I flushed, completely at a loss as to how to proceed.

"You may find when you are in town and as time passes that matters change, and that may be agreeable to you. Your stay here has satisfied me that you are an intelligent young woman, and I do not suppose you are in ignorance of the ways of the world, Mrs Darcy. It is well known, of course, that my nephew keeps a mistress in town. I am afraid I cannot tell you her name, but maybe you can tell me. I can see you are the sort of girl who makes it her business to know matters, and you seem to handle my nephew reasonably soundly, so I shall venture no advice to you."

"And I shall seek none." I looked away from her gaze, intending to show no feeling. A great wave of sickness rose within me, and I was dizzy with the intelligence Lady Catherine had imparted. I was shocked to learn that my marriage had taken place while Mr Darcy was promised to another, but I was blinded by her second revelation. Although she was no friend of mine, she was a woman sharing a womanly confidence, and I had no reason to think her a liar. Why ever would she say such a thing about her own nephew if it were not true?

I thought of the fluttering Mrs Woodham, and of Mrs Lovelace, and the house in Queen Anne's Gate, and the numerous ways and times Fitzwilliam had belittled my origins and family. I thought also of Mama's words to me on the eve of my marriage; she had said my relations with my husband would be short lived and, after the first few weeks of marriage, not oft repeated. Certainly, I knew my parents kept to their own rooms. Even Mary had said Mr Collins only imposed himself upon her once a week. I was suddenly crushed by the realisation that my husband had greater demands, so many, in fact, that he was accustomed to keeping a woman to fulfil them. The betrayal of it overwhelmed me.

"Anne, we must tell Mrs Collins when she visits tomorrow of the letter you have received from Mrs Johnson. She is such a kindly lady to remember the parsonage, and when she visits next month, Mrs Collins shall surely be happy to receive her for tea. I am always pleased to see Mrs Johnson, and she, I know, is wondrous grateful for my condescension, for so she always says."

Lady Catherine's words streamed from her mouth like the babble of a foreign tongue. Anne looked at her satin-covered feet upon the Chinese carpet, and I knew I must get away before the men joined us. I found, from somewhere, the confidence to make a dignified exit.

"I am quite sure my sister will enjoy that Lady Catherine; she is most attentive to these things. Now, if you will excuse me, I find myself very fatigued, and I believe we must start away early tomorrow morning. I think I will retire. I hope I shall have the pleasure of seeing you both at breakfast tomorrow?"

Lady Catherine's eyes narrowed as she beheld my face.

"Yes, Mrs Darcy, certainly. I do not believe in lying abed and would never allow my nephew to leave without a proper farewell."

"In that case, I shall bid you both good night."

Hannah was surprised when I appeared in my chamber, but my manner was brisk, and she ventured no conversation. I did not bathe and was soon dressed in my nightgown, ready to retire.

"Hannah, plait my hair, please."

"Are you certain, madam?"

"Yes." I said no more but stared at my reflection in the mirror as she worked, my face pale in the candlelight. It was not long before Fitzwilliam joined me, but it was long enough for me to arrange myself as if asleep. I curled up, my face turned away, and I made my breathing deep and heavy. I heard bare feet padding around the room as he arrived, and he paused before creeping into bed. The mattress sprang me slightly upwards, and I felt his presence beside me. He whispered my name, but I spoke not. He seemed to hold his breath as he took my plait lightly in his hand and caressed it with his fingers. I knew not his thoughts and could make no sense of him. He was soon asleep whilst I was awake and alone in the darkness.

I FOUND HIM SITTING ON my side of the bed when I awoke. He was fully dressed and looked agitated. "Are you well, Elizabeth? Why did you retire so early? Are you unwell?"

"No, I am fine. I felt rather poorly last night, but I am well now. Is it not time that we were risen? I thought we had to be away early?"

"Yes, well, Fitzwilliam wants to be away early as he has business with his regiment in town this afternoon. But... Elizabeth, are you sure there is nothing wrong?"

"No, there is nothing wrong. All is well," I said as I rose and swept off to my bath, not looking back at him.

The morning passed in attending to practical matters, and I was glad of it. Hannah was anxious for my spirits but too busy packing up my garments and supervising their loading onto our carriage to take up my time. Lady Catherine was at her most friendly at our departure, and even Anne managed a smile as we left her in the shadowy doorway. Despite my poor spirits, I was cheered to know we were departing this place and I would no longer be confined within the home of a woman who disliked me so. That was something to be glad of, and I did my best to focus on it. Knowing we were for town, I had written to my aunt Gardiner and arranged to visit her as soon as may be. My heart sang to think of her and my dear uncle, and I could not see them soon enough.

In the carriage, Mr Darcy and the colonel sat beside one another and I opposite as the Kent countryside rattled by in a riot of green and brown. They spoke of acquaintances in town and Georgiana's newfound confidence. I said little and gazed out of the window until I was forced to speak.

"Well, Lizzy!" boomed Colonel Fitzwilliam. "I must congratulate you on your survival. An Easter at Rosings would be enough to put anyone off the Fitzwilliams, but you have coped admirably. What a wonder it has been to have you with us, to have song at Rosings! I never thought I would hear it, eh, Darcy?"

"Yes, my wife sings very well."

"Indeed you do, Lizzy, but more than that. It was splendid to have some laughter for a change and to have some company beyond Lady Catherine and Anne and this fellow here!" Mr Darcy said nothing at this jibe, and I knew he was annoyed at the colonel's familiarity. I was in no mood to placate him.

"Thank you, Richard. But surely you have never struggled for laughs at Rosings Park, for never was a place so rich in comedy. No, I think if you have not laughed in previous years, then you have only yourselves to blame!" I eyed my husband who did not respond. "And if you have wanted for music, then you could have brought Georgiana with you, for she plays and sings far better than I, and she deserves an audience beyond Mrs Annesley, Fitzwilliam, and me. What say you? Should she join us next year so I can be retired from my position as entertainer?"

"Well, you will have to ask your husband, Lizzy. *He* makes all of the decisions about Georgiana."

Fitzwilliam looked up and almost barked his reply. "Georgiana is terrified of Lady Catherine, Elizabeth. Not all young ladies have your spirit and certainly not Georgiana. If you think you can embolden her to spend two weeks at Rosings, then you have a year to do it, and you must run the risk of her being unhappy."

I smarted at being so censured in front of the colonel, and after the fortnight I had endured with my husband's aunt, I considered it most unjust. "Well, I do not see that Georgiana has anything to fear in Lady Catherine. After all, your aunt likes to have the distinctions of rank preserved and most admires the high-born and the accomplished, does she not? Georgiana surely cannot offend her in any way. *She* is a Fitzwilliam."

"It is Lady Catherine's manner of expressing herself which worries Georgiana, Elizabeth, as you well know. I have protected my sister all her life from situations that may distress her, and I shall not stop now."

"How lucky she is, Mr Darcy," said I, and we spoke no more on the matter.

Chapter Thirteen

The praises heaped upon Mr Darcy's townhouse were not exaggerated. Its towering stucco façade stood behind black railings; within, it held wide hallways and large rooms full of comfortable furnishings and soft colours. There were oil portraits of Darcys past and present, and landscapes aplenty. A splendid pianoforte stood in the drawing room, and the fireplaces were tiled with Italian patterns in all colours. Unlike my aunt and uncle Gardiner's home in Cheapside, Darcy House stood on four floors and somehow felt tall and slim even from the inside. A great oak staircase, carpeted in reds, blues and greens, snaked up the spine of the house. Although I had glimpsed such a place from without, I had never before stepped inside, and in truth, I was impressed. Howsoever that was true, I was certainly not about to tell Mr Darcy.

At breakfast, I asked, "Fitzwilliam, may I have the carriage today, please? I would like to visit my aunt and uncle Gardiner."

"Today? But it is your first day in town, Elizabeth, and we were travelling almost all day yesterday. I am worried you have not been well. Are you sure it would not be best to rest today and visit them tomorrow?"

"No, I would very much like to see them today. I have not seen them these many months."

"Very good. But I need the carriage today as well, so I propose I escort you to your uncle's house and fetch you back this afternoon. Would about three be suitable?"

"Yes, of course. Thank you."

Mr Darcy and I reached Gracechurch Street in little over half an hour.

Joy rose within me as my uncle's red front door came into view, and for very little, I would have danced up the stone steps towards it.

"Will you not come in, Fitzwilliam? You have never met my aunt and uncle Gardiner."

"I am sorry, Elizabeth. I am needed elsewhere on a pressing matter of business. I will be back later." He smiled a weak smile, and I looked away. Fury rose like a fire within me when I thought of his hypocrisy: to keep a woman as he did, to lie to his wife, and still to treat my poor family with disdain.

"Very well." I hardly felt his hand upon mine as he assisted me out of the carriage. My mind was in chaos, and I could find no way forward but to focus on a stream of seemingly inconsequential things. My eyes moved from my slippered feet treading on the iron steps of the carriage to the tapered railings around my uncle's front door. I listened to the calls of an urchin selling wares in the street behind me. I could not look at my husband. But as I lifted my hand to the great brass door knocker, I heard him speak to James: "Yes, Queen Anne's Gate." He saw that the door of my uncle's home had been opened to me and nodded. With no further show of interest, and seemingly eager to get away, he closed the door of the carriage and was gone.

I was undone, and I knew it. Clouds of horrors roared up in my mind. I thought of the shame that he brought on me, of how I loved him, and how little I could reach him. By the time my uncle's butler announced me, I had decided.

"Aunt, I am so sorry; I know I am only just arrived, but I must reach my husband on a matter that cannot be delayed. I have not an instant to lose. But Mr Darcy has the carriage, so may I borrow yours? I shall have it back to you very shortly—within a couple of hours at the most."

Aunt Gardiner's concern was writ upon her face, but she thought I was a sensible girl and so, I believe, assumed I had a sensible reason for my escapade. "Why yes, of course. But, Lizzy, is there really cause to leave directly? Surely, we can send a message to Mr Darcy. Must you go yourself? I shall travel with you."

"No, no, Aunt. There is no need for that, and I would not dream of imposing. No, there is nothing to worry about, but it is an urgent matter. I hope you will forgive me for postponing our tea."

With little further ado, I was in my uncle's carriage, whistling through the narrow streets. What I should do when I got there, I hardly knew, but I was full of righteous indignation, and though I could not say it *to him*, I was full of love—spurned, unreciprocated, unplanned, tormented love. Streets of tall houses seemed to unfold in all directions; the city noise of bartering men and clattering wheels hung in the air. How could it be so loud? Would I ever hear silence again? I sat forward in the seat of the carriage as if I were atop a horse, and I knew that, if I paused or stopped, I might lose my courage. When we arrived in Queen Anne's Gate, I realised I knew not which house I was looking for and was suddenly near collapse with frustration. Our carriage sitting outside a big black door, however, gave Mr Darcy away; almost within one breath, I knocked on it, and I was admitted.

My slippers tapped along a black and white tiled floor as a wigged footman led me forwards. The hush of the interior was a shock after the hum of the street and the banging chaos of my mind. Strange clocks ticked, doors creaked, and within a moment, the footman before me stood aside, announcing, almost to my own surprise, "Mrs Darcy." The room of my reception was large, airy, and hung with colossal oils. Beneath my feet, there was a carpet so thick as to feel like an animal's hide. I held my breath and beheld my husband leaning against a marble fireplace. At his feet, a small spaniel was curled up on the hearthrug, sleeping. Beside him sat a small, grey-haired lady, her bony fingers hovering over a piece of embroidery, a nervous smile playing across her lined face. First, there was silence, and I thought it may never end. The lady before me was at least my mother's age and the scene hardly redolent of misbehaviour. Confused as I was, I was suddenly crushed by the enormity of my error and the impossibility of making it right. What madness had fetched me to such a position as this?

"Mrs Darcy," she said, faintly. "Welcome."

My husband turned away from me towards the wall, raking his fingers through his hair. Knowing I had never been introduced, he seemed to find his composure from somewhere and said, almost in a shout. "Elizabeth, this is Mrs Lovelace, who is a friend of our family. Mrs Lovelace, this is my wife, Mrs Darcy."

"Well, welcome, Mrs Darcy. I was not expecting you, but I am pleased to know you. Are you a happy taker of tea? Please, come closer in order that I can hear you. Please do sit down."

"Thank you, Mrs Lovelace," said I, thoroughly ashamed of myself. I desperately searched for ways to continue the conversation with this elderly woman whom I did not know when I barged uninvited into her home.

"Erm, thank you for your generosity, Esther, but I think Mrs Darcy may be tired, and I suspect we ought to depart," said Fitzwilliam shortly and without looking at me.

"Well, yes of course... then you must go. But I hope to have this pleasure repeated on another occasion. Will you promise me that?"

He blinked as he moved towards me. "Yes, of course. We shall see you again." When Mrs Lovelace's door was closed upon us and we stood outside on the flagstone step, he spoke.

"How did you get here, Elizabeth?"

"I borrowed my uncle's carriage. It is that one on—"

Before I could finish, he approached the driver and spoke words I could not hear. Embarrassment swelled up in me to think of the carriage returning to my aunt and uncle so soon without a passenger or any explanation. Our ride home to Darcy House passed in silence. When he handed me out of the carriage, he did not release my hand but, dismissing all attention from our servants, guided me gently but firmly up the stairs to my bedchamber. Hannah was there when we arrived, but he gave her a look that she could not mistake, and she left without a word.

"Elizabeth, *what are you about?* What on earth were you doing there?"

"What were you doing there, sir? Who is she?"

"Who is she? Who do *you* think she is, Elizabeth?"

"I...I know she is somebody you wish to keep from me... It is for you to tell me the truth, sir, not for me to guess."

"But you must have some idea in your mind of who she is, or you would never have taken such a step. I never would have imagined it of you to behave in such a way. That you would storm into the home of an unknown person, to whom you had no introduction, on a whim that I might be there. What can have been in your mind?"

"I cannot say."

"You can say, Elizabeth, and you will. Tell me now what was in your mind!"

"Very well, if you force me to speak, then *for once* you will hear my honest thoughts! I am not ashamed of what I thought. I had good reason to think it, and it is you who should be explaining yourself, not I! I believed her your mistress, Fitzwilliam. I believed you kept a woman and that Mrs Lovelace was she. I can see I was wrong, but you have still deceived me. You have made me so insecure that I would believe such things of you!"

"I have done no such thing, and you must have taken leave of your senses, Elizabeth. How can you have come to this conclusion? I am responsible for you. I am your husband and protector, and I decide...well, I decide whether certain matters are best kept from you. I assume that, before we were married, you did not challenge your father in this way!"

"What 'certain matters'? What harm can Mrs Lovelace possibly do me? She is an old lady!"

"Yes, she is an old lady, and she can and would do you no harm whatsoever. But it is the fact of her that... Well, now that you have forced yourself into this, you should know, or Lord knows what you will speculate." He sighed heavily and ran his fingers through his hair, turning his angry face away from me and dropping his head slightly.

"Mrs Lovelace is the widow of a neighbour in Derbyshire. She was married and widowed young and left in fairly reduced circumstances. She lost her home in Derbyshire. It was entailed away to her late husband's brother, and he was not well-disposed towards her. She was a respectable woman and known to our family. That was many years ago. For the last twenty years of his life, Esther Lovelace was my father's mistress. He loved her greatly, I believe, and although she does not express her feelings to me explicitly, I rather think that she loved him, too. They have three daughters who are my natural sisters; one has recently married, and you have met her: Mrs Woodham. The house in Queen Anne's Gate was purchased by my father for them to live in when my youngest Lovelace sister, Frances, was a baby. Before that, they lived in another house in town. I believe my father considered the merits of establishing them in Derbyshire but thought they should not be too close to his legitimate family. The rumour was put about that Esther's husband had died on campaign when Frances was a babe, and she had inherited her fortune from a distant relation. I do not believe many people were fooled, and it is very difficult for them to find their way in society. I try to help them as much as possible. Obviously, I provide Esther with an income, and I pay for the house. I provided my eldest sister, Alice, with a dowry when she married Woodham."

"But the Woodhams had only been married for two weeks when we met them at Standenton Park! I can hardly credit you did not tell me this, sir." I was astonished that he had kept the burden of this to himself and that he would arrange this secret world in solitude.

"Yes. But I am torn between helping them and protecting Georgiana and *you*, Elizabeth. I cannot regret having kept this from you, and I cannot see that any respectable gentleman would have done anything else. Alice accosted me at Standenton Park because she wanted an introduction to you, and she knew that, in order to get one, she would have to make it impossible for me to refuse. It was very sly of her, and she knew I was not happy. She is the most assertive of my Lovelace sisters. Sophia and Frances are much more compliant characters."

"I imagine they suit you well, Mr Darcy."

"Yes, they do suit me. I do have affection for them, and I try very hard to help them, but my primary responsibility must be to you and Georgiana. There has been a disagreement recently because Alice—it is always Alice who upsets matters—wants to be introduced to Georgiana as her sister. She wants me to tell Georgiana about them. Sophia, my middle Woodham sister, is very musical, and Alice, having got wind of Georgiana's musical interest, has been using this as an argument in her favour. Even Fitzwilliam agrees and thinks Georgiana could cope with the knowledge of her sisters. But I will not have it. My father kept Esther and the girls separate from his legitimate family, and I shall as well. I have not told you this before in order to protect you, and I do not apologise."

"But I am not your daughter, Fitzwilliam, and I am not an infant sister. I am your wife, and I do not wish to be in ignorance. Why on earth did you not share this with me?"

"Why?" He stared at me, astounded. "Because you are a gently born young woman of not one and twenty, Elizabeth! By God, I am astonished that you even know of such things." He began to storm around the room, his revelations apparently having angered rather than calmed him. "But maybe I should not be surprised. Maybe this sort of thing passes for polite conversation at Longbourn. Maybe young girls in your parents' care are brought up to know every mean crevice of the world. Well, it is not true in my house, Elizabeth, and if I protected you as I would have a daughter of mine protected rather than as your own father may have protected you, then I make no apology!"

Unbidden, tears streamed from my eyes, burning a passage down my flaming cheeks. "No doubt it suits you, sir, to blame my parents for this situation when it is entirely the making of your family. But you are quite wrong. It was, after all, your father who was the author of this 'arrangement.' And as for how I came to believe it, well, it was *your aunt*—whom you are unwilling to speak against even when she criticises everything about me —who told me quite unmistakably that you kept a mistress and that every-body knew. She even said it in front of Anne."

He looked completely stunned, as though the room before him had been removed and he was left in an empty hollow.

"And that is not all she said. She told me, sir, that you were engaged to Anne when you married me, that you were not even free to take me as your wife, and that you *begged* her to forgive you for having betrayed her daughter!" He opened his mouth, but no words came out. I had said so much already that I knew I could not keep silent now. "But it is *my* family who are contemptible, is it not, Mr Darcy? It is *my* family who are so low that I must be denied their company and be shamed and embarrassed at every turn. It is *my* poor sister who must suffer for your arrogance!"

He seemed to recover himself slightly at this and looked at me stern-ly. "Elizabeth, what are you talking about now? I have not the pleasure of understanding you?"

"I speak of your part in Mr Bingley's removing from Netherfield!" I watched as comprehension flickered across his face and waited for him to speak. His silence simply raised my ire further. "You have left me in no doubt, sir, of my inferiority to you, of your attitude to my family and home, and of the degradation in which marriage to me has involved you! You think nothing of the fact that I was forced to marry you with such speed and in such a clandestine way!"

"Forced?" He spoke the word quietly but deliberately, staring straight ahead.

"Yes, 'forced.' For I was offered no choice. You made it plain that you were embarrassed by your connection to me in every way. You spent no time with my family, not even my father. None of your family except Colonel Fitzwilliam attended our wedding, not even Georgiana. Your sister, I was told, was too gently born even to *meet* with my sisters. You kept them away out of shame, and you did not care that I knew your feelings. You did not care for my wishes when you kept me from my sister's wedding because you are ashamed to be connected to her. You escort me to my uncle's home, and you do not even do him the courtesy of meeting him!"

"Elizabeth, please stop."

"No, I will not stop. I have been a good wife to you. I have been the best wife I can be in such circumstances. I have been a kind sister to Georgiana, and I have played hostess to your friends and family. I have visited your tenants and tried to help them when they were in need. When you have kept me away from my family, whom I love, I have not complained of the heartache you caused me. I have welcomed you in my bed night after night. And for all this, you have rewarded me with hardness and deception. I have lived for months knowing that you actually encouraged Mr Bingley out of Hertfordshire and away from my poor sister... and... it is too much for me, and I find I have quite lost my composure."

"I can see that, Elizabeth."

"How could you make so light of it? Why did you remove your friends from my family? And why did you lie to me? You know my sister has a tender regard for Mr Bingley."

"I do not know that, Elizabeth. I observed your sister in Hertfordshire, and although she received his attentions with serenity, I could detect no symptoms of peculiar regard. Her heart looked to me to be not so easily won. The fact that your mother would wish her in love is quite another matter!"

"That is not fair, sir! Mama has nothing to do with Jane and Mr Bingley. The attachment between them is natural. It is not contrived by Mama as ours is!"

"Is that really what you think?" He looked at me—really looked at me as he often did when we were in bed together.

"You give me no reason, sir, to think otherwise. For why else would you be so protective of your friend? You try to prevent his being trapped as you were, but you are unjust, for Jane has done no ill, and she really cares for Mr Bingley. You may have ruined her happiness forever, but you think nothing of it. And as for the relations between you and me, well, I can hardly claim to know your heart. You have never spoken *one word* of love to me."

My eyes stung, and my limbs shook with the weight of what I had said. All the pain and anguish of the last months was spewed upon the floor around me, and I felt trapped. I felt sick to my stomach and dizzy. I knew I had to remove myself from his presence, so I picked up my skirts and ran—ran down the narrow corridor and across the hall, past the gallery, and down the swooping staircase. The gritty light of the London day shone in from the street, and tears blinded my eyes. My heart pounded, and heat rose in every part of me. It happened in a moment: in their haste, my soft slippered feet did not meet the stair, and my shaky hand did not reach the rail, and after a second of crashing confusion and shuddering pain, everything was black.

Chapter Fourteen

A great pain overtook me entirely; it thundered to my fingertips. My eyes were blind, my ears were deaf, and there was nothing in me but a mighty, shattering agony. Sometimes, I knew there were hands and voices, but they signified nothing. My body moved of its own volition. I seemed to stare down a vortex, and the pain in me was so great that I had no words and no will of my own. After the pain, there came colour, and my vision was filled with reds, purples, and blues. The light came at me in an angry manner, and my head could not bear its ferocity, terrifying my senses.

I knew of some things, although not many. I knew of strange hands bending my knees and separating my legs while Hannah whispered I know not what in my ear. I knew of my poor, unwilling body being laid out flat then raised to sit and rolled to the side—and of the endless, sour, stinging vomit. I knew of being hot like a furnace and chilled like a winter dawn. Strange smells passed around my person. I knew of cloths being laid upon my head and along my body and of hands holding mine.

When I opened my eyes, I saw Jane and thought that I was dreaming. She wore her familiar, old, blue muslin, and her flaxen head was bent over a bowl of water. I did not know the bed or the room I was in, but so great was my contentment at her nearness that I simply shut my eyes. At that moment, the door opened, and another person moved about the room.

"Has there been any change, Miss Bennet?"

"I'm afraid not, Mr Darcy, but her temperature is good. She has made some moaning sounds, and she gripped my hand. I am sure it is just a matter of time."

"Thank you," he said quietly. "I hope so." I felt him take my hand and kiss it. "You should rest now, Miss Bennet. You have been up all night, and I would not be able to face your parents if you took ill as well."

"I will rest now that you are here, Mr Darcy, but I am not in such great need. Georgiana sat with Lizzy while I slept for a few hours just after supper, and as you know, you kept the vigil for the whole of the previous two nights as well as during the days."

"Yes, but that was before the fever broke, and so I could not possibly have left her. Those were wretched nights for all of us. No, you have certainly not had enough rest, and you should have some while it offers. If I need help, I have Hannah. And Georgiana. And Miss Lucas is downstairs. Please, go and rest awhile."

"If you put it like that, sir, then I shall." She bent over me and kissed my cheek. She said, "I will be back later, Lizzy," and my senses were full of her soft, rosewater scent. Her feet padded across the carpet, the door clicked, and she was gone. I felt the balance of the mattress change slightly as he leaned on it, still holding my hand, and I could bear to be kept from him no longer. I opened my eyes.

"Elizabeth! Oh, God, Elizabeth!" His handsome face was suffused with a smile. He went to embrace me and then stopped. "I'm sorry; I do not want to hurt you. You must stay still and not exert yourself. I should tell the doctor you are awake, but I do not wish to leave you. Are you in pain?"

I was in pain, but it was not the same as before. When I spoke, each word was a breathy effort. "I feel so tired...I...Where am I?"

"You are in the Rose room in our house in London. It was easier than taking you to your bedchamber, so you have been here. You have been unwell, Elizabeth. You took a fall, and you...you have had a fever. You have been in bed for five days."

I felt a sinking darkness inside and knew there was no life within my body but mine. "I...Am I...Have I?" He seemed to know my meaning and hushed me with his finger against my lips.

"The child was lost, Elizabeth. I am sorry. It was very painful for you, I believe. It was painful for me to watch you, but the doctor says that you have sustained no lasting harm." He spoke what I already knew, and yet it hurt me.

"We have many matters to speak of, Elizabeth, but I am afraid of fatiguing you. Jane is here. Shall I fetch her? She will want to know that you are awake."

I nodded my assent, and he rang the bell. I could not but close my eyes as the door creaked open, for I was once again very weary. Before long, my bedside had further visitors: Jane and a Dr Tranter, who appeared to have been attending me in my woe. After some little discussions with them, I felt unaccountably tired and closed my eyes against the hubbub of their presence. Thus, the time passed in a muddle of people at my bedside and in low conversation in the hall. The sun blazed through the windows then darkness fell. I tasted hot broth and felt arms about me.

When I awoke again, I could not say how many days had passed. I was alone with Jane, and this time, I did not fancy her an apparition.

"Jane?"

"Lizzy!" She rushed to the seat at my bedside and took my hands in hers. "Do not try to get up. I shall fetch you some tea. Now that you are opening your eyes at such short intervals, I assume you are quite well and may start up your old habits."

I smiled, for I could manage nothing more, but inside, I wanted to laugh a loud, throaty laugh and kiss her face. She plumped up my pillows and helped me to sit slightly before presenting me with tea and brushing my hair back from my face.

"How long have I been here?"

"You have been abed for three weeks, Lizzy, but you have only really been conscious for the last two. Even then, it fatigued you so to speak with us that we have not pressed you. You have suffered a severe fever. You took a fall on the stairs, and you were brought here... You... Oh, Lizzy. Do you understand what has happened? Mr Darcy said you did."

"Yes, I knew before he said it. I knew before I knew anything else that my child was dead. How has Mr Darcy been? I feel so wretched, Jane. I had not told him."

She stroked my head and looked me steadily in the eye. "He has said nothing of that, Lizzy. I believe he has simply been worried for you. He has sat up with you most nights."

"How long have you been here?"

"Mr Darcy sent his carriage to Longbourn when you were first taken ill; he asked that I come and bring anyone else I thought might assist your comfort, Lizzy. He wrote that I should choose and that my judgement would be the right judgement. He said all of our family could come or just me—whatever I thought best. As it is, Lydia is away to Brighton, and Mama has been poorly herself, so she keeps Kitty busy at home. I asked Charlotte Lucas to accompany me, so she is here as well. We have cared for you separately and together, and sometimes Miss Darcy has sat with you. She has been here for about a week. She has a sweet disposition, but I do not believe she is one for the sick room, Lizzy."

I smiled at this description of Georgiana. "No, indeed. I hope that she has not been too worried."

"If I am any judge, I think she has been quite sleepless with anxiety. But she is happy now that you have awakened, and Dr Tranter has said you will improve each day."

"I do not quite feel myself. I feel very weak indeed."

"That is to be expected, Lizzy. You have had a very bad fever. But each day you will get better than the last, and you will feel yourself again; I know you will."

The door crept open as if pushed by a kitten, and Hannah appeared. "Miss Bennet, Mr Darcy thought you may wish to know that Mr Bingley and his sister are arrived. They are taking tea in the drawing room if you wish to join them. I can take over here, miss."

"Thank you, Hannah." Jane did not look at all surprised by this intelligence. "I shall come down directly. Lizzy, I shall leave you for half an hour. Do you mind?"

"Of course not. It will be just what you need to see Mr Bingley again."

"It will, well…it has been. This is not the first time he has called. He has called twice already during the time I have been here caring for you although this is the first time Caroline has joined him. I do not know *she* is just what I need, but I shall keep an open mind." She smiled lightly, and a person who did not know her, might miss her joke.

"Go. Enjoy your tea and your Mr Bingley."

I realised upon listening to Hannah that I had been hearing her voice almost constantly; I suspected she had barely left my bedside during my illness. Now that I was awake and we were alone, she was calm and unassuming, busying herself with folding linens and changing water.

"If you are not too tired, madam, I think we ought to change your nightgown."

I said I was feeling quite alert, and so she assisted me to the side of the bed, and there I sat, feeling the cool air on my skin. She gently removed my old gown, which, although I was no longer feverish, was damp from the heat of my body. Hannah was unaffected by my nakedness, but I was shocked and mortified to see I was thinner under my clothes, that my hipbones protruded slightly, and that my bosom was shrunken.

"Oh, Hannah, I do not look well. I can see my bones!"

"Well, you have been ill for three weeks, madam, and could only eat a very little. We will fatten you back up I am sure with Cook's good offerings."

"But my bosom! None of my dresses will fit, and what will Mr Darcy say? In fact—" An awful thought occurred to me. "Has Mr Darcy already seen these changes?"

"The master has been in almost constant attendance on you. He has sat with you for almost all of the time you have been in this bed, but I do not believe he has seen you unclothed. No. I have changed your gowns, sometimes with assistance from Miss Bennet, but nobody else has seen you thus. In any case, Mr Darcy has been very anxious for you, madam. If I may be so bold, I believe he would not care about your reduced bosom."

"Oh, Hannah, he might." I struggled with myself for a moment, wondering how much to tell her. "Just before I fell ill, well, I quarrelled with Mr Darcy. I fear he may not be able to forgive me. And in addition to that, I had not even told him I was with child. I dread to think what opinion he must have of that! And if I am less comely as well as having committed these offences… well, it may be that he does care. Oh Hannah, what am I to do?"

"I think that you must not concern yourself with these worries, madam. I thought that you must have quarrelled because of the way he dismissed me from your chamber when you arrived home that awful day. Then I heard you cry out and ran to the stairs, and I noticed your face was much stained with tears, so I thought you must have been crying before you fell. So yes, I had suspected you had had some sort of disagreement with the master, but whatever it was about, madam, he could not have attended you more constantly, and so I feel sure that it is forgotten."

"But what about the baby, Hannah? I had not even told him to expect it!"

"I am sure, madam, that he was most concerned for you. And in truth, everything happened so quickly, with so many people running hither and thither, that there was little time for discussion."

"I want you to tell me about it. I want you to tell me what nobody else will."

She paused and seemed to consider my request. "I can if you insist, madam. But I think that it might be better saved for another time? When you have been recovered for a few weeks maybe? When you feel more yourself?"

I wondered at this and considered the virtues of not hearing the truth until later and having more time to gather my strength. Although, in some respects, I was afraid of what had happened during my illness, I yearned and longed to have it within my knowledge. "No, Hannah, I would like to know now."

"Very well, in that case, I beg that we dress you first." I acquiesced in this suggestion and felt the clean sharpness of freshly laundered cotton sliding across my body.

"I got to you first, but Mr Darcy was already halfway down the stairs." She said this and, sitting beside me on the bed, clasped her hands in her neat lap before continuing. "You were in a heap at the bottom. Nobody knows how many you fell down, but you must have knocked your head as you were not conscious of us, madam. I called to you, and you responded not. The master embraced you and spoke to you, but you did not open your eyes. By this time, a number of others had arrived—James and one of the footmen and the head housemaid. The master had sent James away to fetch a physician directly, and he continued to hold you and speak to you, asking you to open your eyes. It was then that I noticed blood upon your skirts and upon your slippers."

"So soon after the fall?" My mind reeled, and I almost wretched from the implications of this. "What did the master say?"

"He said little at first, madam. I saw his face at the moment he saw the blood, and I believe that he was confused and anxious. As to how much he understood, I could not say. He is a man, and...well...I have witnessed a loss before, madam. I attended my sister when she lost a child, so I knew immediately. I said that I thought we needed to get you to a bed as quickly as may be. Mr Darcy agreed, and he carried you to this room, which was the nearest. We laid you out on the bed, and he cradled your head while I removed your slippers and stockings and...well...checked that the blood was flowing from you as I thought it was. It was, madam, and when Dr Tranter arrived, he did not need to be told. He asked outright how far along you were, and I quickly answered that I believed about four months. Dr

Tranter warned us then that a loss at four months could be long and hard, and so it was. After a little time, you awoke, madam, but you were in grave pain, I believe. The worst part of the bleeding was a long business. Dr Tranter attended you from time to time. I remained here and dealt with the blood and tried to get you to drink small amounts of weak tea. Mr Darcy said very little, but he remained here with you, holding your hand. The master said nothing then or later except that, when the worst of the bleeding was over, he looked at me, steady like, and thanked me. I thought that he meant to thank me for answering the physician's questions when he could not have done so, but I cannot be sure. Maybe I presume too much."

"I am sure you do not. Oh, Hannah, how wretched I feel. How appalled he must have been to learn about my condition in that way and then to see me in such straits. To know his child was paying the price of my foolhardy actions. It was Mr Darcy who told me when I awoke that I was no longer with child, but I hardly dare to discuss it further with him."

She said nothing more on the matter but urged me not to think on it.

MANY DAYS PASSED HENCE. PEOPLE came in and out of my presence, and in sleep and wakefulness, I came in and out of theirs. Charlotte fed me broth and told me of the latest news from Lucas Lodge. To hear her voice was a tonic. Georgiana sat beside me, fidgeting and speaking of Pemberley. She cried on her first visit and kissed my cheek declaring, "Oh, Lizzy, I thought you were dead." On one afternoon, I awoke to find my aunt Gardiner sitting beside me, her fingers working her embroidery, her intelligent eyes darting around. She kissed me as I woke and smiled a knowing smile.

"Aunt."

"Lizzy. Shh. Do not tire yourself, my love. I shall stay with you for the rest of the day, and if sleep is what you need, then you should take it."

"Oh, Aunt, I am sorry about the last time we met! I can hardly credit that I—"

"Hush, Lizzy. There is nothing for which you need apologise. Think not on the matter. Would you like some tea?"

With that, she set about pouring tea and ensuring I was comfortable. She told me the news from Gracechurch Street: how my cousins fared and how my uncle was so busy with his business that he could scarce draw breath. They had already despaired of having any time for a holiday this year and were resigned to remaining at home throughout the summer. Mr Darcy, I was given to understand, had written express to Gracechurch Street when I was ill and then visited in person once my fever had broken.

"I must say, Lizzy, Mr Darcy was very agreeable to us on his visit to Cheapside. He was all that was polite and kind, and for such an august man, well, he had no false dignity at all. It was...well, it was not quite what I had been led to expect from him after all that your uncle and I had heard from Longbourn. He and I found common ground in our memories of Lambton. Your uncle looks forward to the fishing he has been promised at Pemberley, although I understand that that must wait until next summer. We are looking forward to Christmas in Derbyshire with you very much."

I was all astonishment. "Mr Darcy has invited you to Pemberley for Christmas?"

"Yes. Were you not aware? Are you not pleased, Lizzy?"

"Yes, of course, I am pleased. I am so thrilled that I shall wish away the year." I sank back on my pillows and wondered at what could have wrought such a change in my husband.

Jane was my most constant attendant. She spoke sparingly of Mr Bingley's visits, but I knew that she enjoyed them greatly. She also related the news from Longbourn—that the regiment had departed and encamped at Brighton for the summer, and that our sister Lydia, much to Papa's vexation, had been invited to join them by Mrs Forster, the young wife of the colonel of the regiment. I could not imagine that this was wise, but I amused myself with visions of Lydia making a spectacle of herself by the sea. Fitzwilliam sat with me every day and in the evening until I slept. He had selected various books from the library that he read to me sometimes rather sleepily. We did not speak of our baby or the things we had said to each other on the day of my fall, and I did not know when we would.

Chapter Fifteen

When I expressed a wish to leave my sickroom, my husband carried me downstairs to the parlour. I was quite capable of walking, but when his strong arms came under my knees and behind my neck, I needed to feel them. I felt the old familiar desire for contact with his body and could not give it up when offered. At other times, we sat in the courtyard garden in dappled sunlight, our hands touching. We spoke little, but I found such harmony in the nearness of him that I was afraid to break the spell with words. Eventually, my old curiosity and restlessness got the better of me.

"We must have some conversation, Mr Darcy, but very little will suffice," I said one afternoon when we sat in the garden alone.

"What would you speak of Elizabeth?"

I thought of the matter that most concerned me but could not find the courage to mention it. I ventured into safer territory. "Mr Bingley calls a great deal. When did you inform him that we were returned to town?"

"I do not believe that I ever did exactly inform him. I sent him a message that your sister was here as our guest, and it was then that he began his daily visits. I do not think that you or I have much to do with it, Elizabeth."

I leaned over to him and kissed his cheek. "Thank you, Fitzwilliam."

"Not that he is unconcerned for your health, of course."

"Of course." I shot him a conspiratorial smile. "Jane told me of your message to her and your consent to bring all our family with her if she thought it best. I thank you for that, Fitzwilliam. It was very civil of you."

"I hope civility is not something you ever need to ask for again, Elizabeth.

When I think of my relations with your family…well…I am heartily ashamed. I never thought of how it would injure you to be so separated from them. I never considered that I would not be enough for you, and I regret that very much. I have been very selfish and full of pride where you are concerned. Of course, you must see your family as often as need and affection dictate. When you fell ill, I knew you would need your sister, and that is why I sent for her."

"I did need her, but maybe we are all fortunate she did not bring Mama with her?"

"Well, maybe, but your mother is welcome in our home as well, Elizabeth."

"Thank you. It is very good of you to show so much consideration to her. It shows some greatness of spirit, I think, with all that happened."

He looked nervously down as if between breaths. "Elizabeth… I have wanted to, well, I think there are certain things we ought to discuss, but I am anxious not to tire you or make you unwell. I never thought to argue as we did before your fall, and there were things you said then which *troubled* me greatly and… Well, if they *are* true or you *believe* them to be true, then I have served you very ill. If you are up to it, maybe we can start with this matter of your mother. What do you mean when you say 'all that happened'?"

It was a simple question, and I concluded in the following moment of silence that it was best met with a simple answer. We had each dissembled enough. "I mean that my mother observed you speaking with me in private, affected to have observed you kissing me, and you were thereby forced to marry me when you had intended no such thing. If you have found me a tolerable companion, then I suppose you have been lucky. Under the circumstances, I am blessed that you are a kind husband. I hope we have reached some sort of understanding and we can continue to live happily, but if you think I forget the manner in which you were obliged to do it, then you are mistaken."

"Is that really your opinion of matters? That is how you interpret what happened in Hertfordshire? How you must have suffered all these months."

"What other interpretation is there?"

"Well, there is the interpretation that I married you because I love you." He paused and his words settled upon the air like a summer scent. "Almost from the first moments of our acquaintance, I came to feel for you a passionate affection and regard which, despite the position of your family as

compared with mine, I could not repress. By the time of the ball at Netherfield, I was quite lost to you, Elizabeth. The thought of your being taken in
by Wickham…still more…admiring him—"

"Fitzwilliam, I did not—"

"No, let me speak my fears now that I have started. The thought of your
admiring him…well… I could not bear it. I resolved to speak with you at
the ball, but as you know, we were soon in debate on the matter. When I
took you into that salon, I had no intention of compromising you; of course,
I did not. But…well, Elizabeth…in the moment your mother approached…
when we were alone and I could feel your nearness, I wanted to kiss you very
much. I hardly know what I would have done given a few moments more. I
came to think Mrs Bennet saw something that was real even if she did not
describe it exactly as it was. She is not a fool, Elizabeth, and although she
was not completely truthful, she was not a liar either."

I sank back in my chair, and my lips formed a wordless "O."

"As you know, things developed very quickly as they always do when a
gentleman believes that his daughter has been compromised. I could not
blame your father for wanting the matter concluded. In any case, it suited
me. I did not wish to linger with your family, whom I mistakenly and
proudly considered beneath me. I also wanted you as my wife, Elizabeth.
At the time, it seemed as though fate had offered me the perfect scenario.
But I was wrong to act as I did. I should have courted you properly in front
of your family and friends, and I should have married you after a period of
engagement with your family and mine in attendance. You should have had
time to have a dress made. It was my fault that you did not, Elizabeth, and
I hope that one day you can forgive me my pride and arrogance."

"What of the Bingley party? If you are in earnest, then I cannot understand why you sent Mr Bingley away."

"Of that I am deeply ashamed, Elizabeth. Bingley's sisters came to me
early on the morning after the ball, before I set off for Longbourn. Of course,
they did not know what had passed between you and me—or what was
alleged to have passed between us. Your father and I had done a creditable
job of hushing up the whole matter. I did this because I did not want you
to be embarrassed by scandal. Of course, it also had the unintended consequence that Bingley's sisters did not understand my entanglement with
your family at that point. They had observed their brother and your sister

during the ball and took the view that he was about to make her an offer. Frankly, they wanted to stop it. As I did at the time, they held a poor opinion of your family. I realise now that they were also jealous of Jane—jealous of her beauty and goodness. For my part, I suspected your mother had pushed Jane in the path of Mr Bingley. I also feared—and I am ashamed when I think of it—that were Jane to marry Bingley, it would make it harder for me, as your husband, to keep your family at bay. And so I agreed to help them persuade him to town. I am not proud of this history, Elizabeth."

I realised he had confessed to sins he could have kept concealed, and I was greatly touched. How like him to do more than was really necessary. In any case, did I not have my own transgressions for which I must atone?

"And I am not proud of my visit to Mrs Lovelace. At least you have tried to mend the situation of Jane and Mr Bingley."

"Elizabeth, you have been unwell, and there is no need for you to worry about Esther. She will not have been offended. Let us leave it at that. Lady Catherine is another matter. I do not really know what to do about her. I have been focusing my mind on you and your recovery. But at some time, I shall have to face her. I cannot let it pass after what she has said to you."

"I will leave it up to you, Fitzwilliam. I cannot claim any knowledge of your aunt which would enable me to assist you."

"No, well, I am not sure anyone would. The truth is there never was any engagement to Anne. It was all a fiction of Aunt Catherine's mind. She always had her heart fixed on my marrying Anne, and she was angry when I married you without informing her. She wrote me a very intemperate letter, but when I wrote back, she replied she would accept you, and she hoped I would visit Rosings at Easter as normal, so I thought all was mended. Obviously, I was wrong. But still, for her to say such a thing to you and to tell you I kept another woman…well, I can hardly credit it."

"Would Colonel Fitzwilliam have any notion of how to approach the matter?"

"I doubt it. He has never had to face up to Lady Catherine. He has never done anything that displeases her, and frankly, she is less concerned with him than she is with me. In any case, I would not share something like this with my cousin. It is too close to us—to our marriage—for him to be involved."

"Is this related at all to your dislike for 'Richard' and 'Lizzy'?"

"No. Well, yes, a little. Fitzwilliam and I have always been close. I know

him, and...well, he likes you too much, Elizabeth, and in the wrong way."
He did not look at me as he said this but down at his lap. My naiveté, I
realised, had been great.

"I see. You must forgive me for not catching these things. Had I ever
been courted, I might be better equipped."

His face spread with a smile, and he touched my belly. "I am courting
you now, Elizabeth, from the safety of our marriage."

"Of course, it may help you with your cousin should you call me 'Lizzy'
as well. After all, Georgiana and all of my family do, and then there would
be an equality of arms."

"But I like 'Elizabeth.'"

His voice was heavy with passion as he said my name, and I realised in
that moment that it always had been thus. The air had become slightly chilly,
and the light was ebbing. When I thought of the words he had spoken, I
felt light in my body. My heart sang at the knowledge of his love. Tired as
I was, I reached out my hand to him and touched his cheek. We had not
discussed everything, but we had made a start.

"I am growing a little weary, Fitzwilliam."

"Of course; I will take you in."

"Thank you...but...well, since I am so much better, do you not think it
time for me to return to my own chamber?" I hoped my meaning was plain.

"I suppose, if you wish it, then you should, but it is easier for Jane and
Miss Lucas to attend to you in the Rose room as that is closer to their
chambers—"

"But I am past the stage of requiring people to sit with me all night
and...in any case...I shall have you, shall I not?"

"Yes, you shall, Elizabeth, if you want me. I...I have been worried you
thought it something of a sacrifice."

"I did not. And you cannot really have thought that, not when you know
how I have given myself to you, surely, Mr Darcy?"

"Well... Since the night after the highwaymen, I have known that we...
well...that we...well, I certainly have never felt more fulfilment than in
your arms, Elizabeth." He looked at me steadily but nervously and said,
not quite daring to make it a question, "I hoped that you were happy when
you were in mine."

"I was. I always was. If it is not an imposition, sir, I would return to them."

With little further discussion, Mr Darcy offered me his arm. I returned, as if I had never been away, to my own chamber. The room I had run from in tears and torment, I re-entered in calmness and love. Hannah assisted me in my bath and brushed my hair. As usual, she anticipated me. "Shall I leave your hair loose this evening, madam?"

"Yes please, Hannah."

She helped me into one of my fine ivory nightgowns and left me sitting at my vanity, pondering my reflection in the mirror. My eyes surveyed my slighter figure and shrunken bosom. I tried breathing in and thrusting my chest out to only minimal effect.

"Elizabeth, what are you doing?"

I spun around to see Fitzwilliam in the doorway, still dressed and grinning.

"I fear that I am rather thin now, Fitzwilliam, and I have become flat around my chest. I was attempting to disguise it, but I confess the only remedy is Cook's fine cuisine!"

He ran his finger across the exposed part of my bosom, holding my gaze in the mirror. "I am not sure that I would say *flat*—a little less full maybe. But you must know, you are still exquisite, Elizabeth. In any case, these things will pass, especially if your appetite continues as it has this last week."

"You speak as if that does not please you?"

"You know everything about you pleases me."

To see him standing before my bed in the half-light of the summer dusk reminded me with a jolt that, in my recklessness, I had lost our child, and I was overcome with sadness. An ache deep within me seemed to roar. "That cannot be true, Fitzwilliam." I decided to speak while I had courage. "It cannot please you that I lost your child. It cannot please you that I kept it from you and that I behaved so rashly, that—"

"Hush, Elizabeth. You must never think of what has happened in that light." He knelt beside me and took me in his arms. "It is not so. The doctor assured me that it... well... it would have happened eventually. The child was not meant to be, Elizabeth. He or she... it was not your fault. I hope you can accept that. I accept it. I certainly could never blame you. You have suffered so much, and I know you are not at fault. As for your not having told me you were with child... well... I am ashamed of myself that you did not feel able to approach me. You said I had not spoken one word of love to you, and I realise now that I had not. A man who felt less might have said more. But I say it now, very clearly. I have come to realise that I have been altogether too silent with you. I have not told you what is in my mind, and I have made you shy of speaking truth to me. Know this. You are the wife of my choice, and I love you."

Tears stung my eyes, and a shiver crept across my back. He picked me up and took me to my bed, undressing and joining me in a trice. Quietly, gently, beneath the cover, he loved me, and I loved him with all that was in me. As he reached fulfilment, he said my name. He whispered, "I love you" into the crook of my neck as he lay, spent, above me, and I knew he meant it. I could feel my eyelids closing and the energy leaving me, but still he stroked my shoulder.

"You know that I also love you, Fitzwilliam."

"I hope so. I hope very much that it is so."

"Of course, it is so. I would never have gone to Mrs Lovelace's if I had not loved you."

He planted a kiss on my head and whispered, "I know. Sleep." And I slept.

Chapter Sixteen

When the time came for Jane to return home, I felt none of the dread at the prospect of being separated from her as I had felt upon our last parting. I had been blessed with her company for four glorious weeks, and during that time, she had quite restored me. Of course, I ached when I thought of my poor child, but in body, I was back to health. The summer had drawn on and grown stifling in the close streets of town. We had never intended to stay away from Pemberley so long, and it was only concern for my health that kept Fitzwilliam from ordering our immediate departure for Derbyshire. Jane's final full day with us was a sultry one, and we spent it lazily, walking in Hyde Park under the shade of parasols and talking in the hazy sunlight of the courtyard garden at Darcy House. The evening was set aside for a trip to the theatre with Mr Bingley, his sisters, and our aunt and uncle Gardiner, so Jane and I were quite determined to make the most of our time together during the day. Glasses of elderflower cordial glistened between us, and we talked.

"Mr Darcy seems a most devoted husband, Lizzy. I shall be glad to tell Mama when I return and mean it. I know she was rather anxious."

"Yes, he is. I am very lucky, Jane. But I must say that I wonder at Mama! I knew that she was worried for me as Mary said so, and as you rightly say, there is no need to be. But, well, I cannot be touched by it when she forced me into marriage with Mr Darcy, not knowing him for the man he truly is. After all, she did not know on my wedding day that he would be kind."

"No, perhaps not, but he is, isn't he? Lizzy, he is kind to you *when you are between yourselves,* I hope?"

I could hear the strain in her voice and knew she may have spent days and weeks thinking of how to broach this subject with me. Like me before my marriage, she was ill-informed of the facts, and she was mortified with embarrassment.

"Yes." I laughed slightly. "He certainly is. He is very kind. And Jane, when you come to marry and Mama speaks to you of *those things* the night before, take little notice of what she says. She exaggerates and is not very comforting on the subject. When the time comes, I shall talk to you."

Jane flushed. "Thank you, Lizzy—although, you will have to approach me as I could never ask about that! In any case, nobody has offered for me, so we are safe from embarrassing conversations yet awhile. But you must promise me that you hold nothing against our mother. After all, if Mama acted rashly over the matter, then maybe you should be glad she did?"

"Jane, you are too good. Mama does not deserve you. My only wish is that you find the felicity in marriage that I have. Mr Bingley still visits, I see. And of course, we have tonight."

"Now you sound like Mama yourself. I hope that I do not have to guard against false accusations of familiarity this evening!"

"I doubt that will be necessary. I see how Mr Bingley looks at you. We all do. But has he said anything about returning to Netherfield?"

"No, he has not, although he does say often how happy he was there. I cannot imagine what keeps him in town in this hot weather."

"Can you not?"

We exchanged a quick and affectionate look. "No, Lizzy. That is ridiculous. I am sure that he does not remain in town simply to call at this house. That is quite silly. After all, he stayed away from Netherfield for so many months when I was but three miles from the threshold. No. He must have business here or something of that nature."

"Well, we shall see," said I, knowing better than to push my sister's modesty.

We took a light luncheon with Georgiana, and the rest of the day passed in a languid haze of theatre preparation and friendly gossip. When the evening came, Hannah dressed me in a pale pink silk gown that I had never worn before and adorned my hair with tiny roses. My first evening out in town as Mrs Darcy had arrived, albeit eight weeks after I had arrived myself, and I was agog with excitement. Jane wore blue and looked a great beauty. Georgiana was always well dressed and did not disappoint her audience. I believe Mr Darcy was quite content to escort the three of us into his carriage and up the marble steps of the theatre. The place was a throng of fashionable faces, fluttering fans clasped by jewelled fingers, and flapping coattails on eminent gentlemen. I heard snatched whispers of "Mrs Darcy" and "girl from Hertfordshire" on the air as I passed unknown loiterers, but I cared not. Our aunt and uncle Gardiner, Mr Bingley, Miss Bingley, and Mr and Mrs Hurst met us in the box and were all, for their various reasons, delighted to be there. Miss Bingley and Mrs Hurst, I believe, liked to be seen in Mr Darcy's box and seemed to remain standing for an unnecessarily long time. Mr Bingley immediately took charge of Jane, conducting her to her seat and engaging her in conversation that we all knew would consume both for the evening. Our aunt and uncle were, I believe, simply pleased to see Jane and me together, happy and healthy.

"My dear, Eliza," heralded Miss Bingley. "How wonderful to see you —and looking quite recovered! I would have expected a country girl such as yourself to be more robust. But maybe it was all the travel you have been undertaking. I understand you visited Kent from Pemberley and then to town when I suppose you are not used to such long journeys. And to be in town for so many weeks but not able to go out must have been a real trial—"

Mr Darcy cut her off sharply. "Thank you, Miss Bingley. Fortunately, Mrs Darcy is quite recovered; however, I will not have her health discussed before the whole of London. And as for not going out before tonight—perhaps, I have been unwilling to share my wife with others."

With that, she was silent. He conducted me to my seat, sat next to me, and as the theatre darkened for the performance, I leaned to his ear and whispered, "Thank you, sir. If you should become any more demonstrative in public, I should hardly know you."

"I hope you do not come to expect it, Elizabeth. It is quite against my nature. But on this occasion, I felt one comment would be sufficient."

With that, I relaxed into my chair and revelled in the opera.

We were a jolly party on the way home. Jane and I had never attended such a well-appointed theatre and never in such finery. We had been to smaller performances with Aunt and Uncle Gardiner, but the evening's entertainments had been quite outside our experience, and we were giddy with excitement. I wondered that Jane was not a little agitated as she fixed me with an extravagant smile from across the carriage. I thought no more of it and enjoyed our ride home in the slightly cooler air of the night. Upon our return, we clattered into the lobby of the house. Cloaks were unbuttoned, hats removed, and contentment expressed by all. I believe Jane and Georgiana were shocked when Mr Darcy responded to my yawns by picking me up in his arms, turning to them to say, "Goodnight ladies," and then proceeding up the stairs. For myself, I was neither shocked nor unhappy. I gripped his lapels and kissed his ready mouth as soon as we were out of sight.

"Hannah, you may retire. I will attend to your mistress this evening," he said as he deposited me on the bed.

"Yes, sir."

I smiled at Hannah and thanked her with my eyes, suddenly conscious that, as a maiden, she was sometimes party to things she should not be. When she was gone, my husband kneeled on the end of the bed and removed my tiny satin slippers whilst stroking the arches of my feet.

"It was wonderful to see you enjoying yourself this evening, Elizabeth, but I must confess, I have passed the entire evening anxious to get you home."

"Whatever for, sir?" I teased as his hands crept up my legs and found my stocking tops.

"Well, firstly, to do this," said he as he pulled each stocking down, discarding them either side of the bed. "And secondly, to do this." He pushed up my skirts and began to kiss the inside of my knees and thighs, his hands reaching up the bodice of my dress. His grip was strong, and his kiss was hot against my skin. My back arched, and a passion for him shuddered through my body. When I could bear his ministrations no longer, I sat up and ran my fingers through his dark curls, bringing his face to mine, savouring his breath as he began to work on the buttons at the back of my dress. He said my name almost in a whisper as I kissed his neck, but in that moment, we were startled by a light tap upon the door. "Shh," I said as I covered his mouth with my hand, alarmed that somebody stood outside of my chamber. We waited in silence, our passion arrested, until there came another tap and Jane's lilting voice rang out. "Lizzy, are you there?"

"I shall come directly, Jane. In just one minute!"

Mr Darcy looked at me in astonishment.

"If I did not answer, then she would worry, Fitzwilliam, and I cannot send her away without seeing her!"

"And where shall I go?" he asked slightly above a whisper. He was poised above me, aroused and dishevelled, and I knew it would not do for my sister to see him.

"Go into your chamber, Fitzwilliam. I will come and tell you when she has gone." With that, he stole through the connecting door as I slid off the bed and made some effort to straighten my skirts. Jane entered, and as her eye passed over me to my bare feet, and the discarded slippers, and stockings on the floor, she blushed.

"Oh, I am sorry, Lizzy, I should not have come. I . . . I just had to tell you. I could not sleep without telling you. *Mr Bingley has asked for my hand, Lizzy!*"

"Oh, Jane!" I embraced her and kissed her cheek, my bare toes and rumpled appearance quite forgotten in my joy at her news.

"He will follow us to Hertfordshire the day after tomorrow and, when he is arrived at Netherfield, call upon Papa directly! Oh, Lizzy, I can scarcely credit that things would end in this happy way!"

"Well, I am not at all surprised. Did I not say it would be so? But how shall you keep this to yourself before he calls at Longbourn? You shall go distracted with the effort!"

Jane confessed that she had not thought of that, and we spoke of many things—of church bells, and wedding breakfasts, and the giddiness of love. By the time she left, completely fatigued by excitement and the lateness of the hour, I was conscious that my husband had been waiting far longer than he may have anticipated. I found him slumped in a chair by his bed, ostentatiously fingering a book, which I knew he was not reading.

"Oh, Fitzwilliam, you will never guess Jane's news!"

"I imagine that I will, Elizabeth. Bingley has asked her to marry him."

"Is it not wonderful? I am overjoyed for her."

I could see at a glance that Fitzwilliam was not as overwhelmed as I. Knowing he was still smarting from his unceremonious ejection from my chamber and suddenly desirous of his touch, I sat upon his lap and kissed his face by the light of the moon.

THE MORTIFICATION AND EMBARRASSMENT OF my visit to the home of Mrs Lovelace prayed heavily on my mind, and for that reason, I petitioned my husband for us to visit her once more, this time together. I tackled him on the matter one afternoon as we completed our luncheon. We sat at right angles on the corner of the dining room table, empty plates and drained glasses between us. Fitzwilliam was most reluctant for such a meeting to occur. I believe he had hoped I would change my mind.

"You must understand there is no need for this escapade, Elizabeth. I am quite sure Esther was not offended and…well, I would not wish you to make yourself uncomfortable or to remind yourself of that dreadful day and how you must have felt. I would rather leave the matter alone."

"I cannot really countenance that, Fitzwilliam. After all, I did descend upon her home without invitation or introduction when you were there on a private matter. It was terribly rude. Heaven knows how I appeared to her, and I felt she was quite gracious under the circumstances. I feel I ought to see her again to make my peace and to ensure she knows I bear her no ill will. She and her daughters are your family, after all, if not your legitimate one. I would not wish to become a problem between you, even an unspoken one."

"You are astonishing, Elizabeth. You amaze me, my love. Many, I may say most, married women would not take that attitude. Do you realise that?"

I sighed and straightened my knife and fork on my plate. The truth of his words, I knew very well. Scandal had long arms, and Mrs Lovelace had been embroiled in scandal for almost all of her adult life. I doubted whether my mother or my aunts would wish to take tea with a woman who had lived *unmarried* with a man for twenty years and borne him three children. I knew they would not. I thought of Mrs Lovelace's jittery fingers over her embroidery and the fluttering hands of Mrs Woodham and suddenly understood these were women who suffered greatly at the hands of society's disapproval.

I placed my hand over my husband's and answered him. "Yes I do, but she is an old lady. It would surely be wrong to treat her with anything less than civility because she was a man's mistress in her youth. Is to understand all not to forgive all?"

"It lasted two decades, Elizabeth. Many people die before they have been married for twenty years. It was a long time. Its legacy is that most respectable people will have nothing to do with her. She has money, and she has the girls, but she wants for society in general. Frankly, she is a social outsider. Esther did not look for scandal; it happened to her. And once it had started, it could not be stopped. She is a prisoner of her history, so I think she would very much like to know you. But I will not have you feeling obliged, and I will not encourage them in this quest for the girls to know Georgiana."

I considered this silently for a moment. My own view was that, as she grew older, Georgiana ought to know of her sisters, but Fitzwilliam was excessively protective of her. He seemed determined to keep her in a state of childlike ignorance of the world, which I thought ill advised and doomed to failure. After all, Georgiana would be coming out herself next year. How could she be shielded from the ways of the world and closed off from gossiping tongues?

"Well, it need be just a short visit—only Mrs Lovelace, you, and I. Would that satisfy your scruples, sir?"

"I expect it must. I do not believe you will take no for an answer in this, Elizabeth; am I right?"

"You are, I am afraid." I rose from my seat and kissed him lightly on the cheek by way of thanks for his indulgence. I buttered a piece of bread and cut it on my plate, silver tinkling on pretty china. There were no servants in the room, and I saw my chance. "Fitzwilliam, did your mother know?"

"I believe she did, yes. I never discussed the matter with her, of course, and never would have done so. As it was, I did not know myself until after her death. My father informed me himself when I was one and twenty. He was in ill health by that time and, I believe, was feeling his own mortality keenly. In addition, he thought that, as a man, I should know. I cannot approve of it, but as I said to you before, I believe he loved Esther. I cannot know of what my mother was aware. It seems likely she knew some, if not all, of the truth. It was a lamentably well-known state of affairs amongst society generally. And of course, other family members certainly knew. Lord and Lady Matlock know who the Lovelaces are, and I know they would not consort with them. Aunt Mary did notice Alice at the Standenton Park ball, and she was appalled. She upbraided me for not preventing your dancing with Woodham and for not walking away from Alice when she accosted us. She said I was not protecting you as I should. They certainly are not the only ones who know. I can only think that the truth of my father's situation inspired Lady Catherine to say what she said to you. Fitzwilliam knows of course, but he would have no objection to meeting any of them. He is, as you know, a man of easy attitudes, and he takes people as he finds them."

"Yes, yes, he does. What does the colonel think about this business of introducing Georgiana to her sisters?"

"I regret to say, Elizabeth, that he is all in favour of it."

"Really?" What a sensible man my husband's cousin is.

"Yes, really. I am astounded at him. He who *knows* how sensitive Georgiana is. I believe it would be quite disturbing for her."

I let the matter pass, believing I would be more persuasive once I had met properly with Mrs Lovelace and corrected my mistake. And so, it was resolved that Fitzwilliam and I would call at Queen Anne's Gate together in two days' time. He looked at me doubtfully as he sat down at his desk to pen Mrs Lovelace a warning, but he did it all the same, and I was glad.

While he worked, I passed the time reading by his side then arranging new summer flowers in the parlour and the music room. A flurry of letters arrived from Longbourn announcing Jane's engagement to Mr Bingley, and even Charlotte wrote to assure me that Meryton, as one, spoke of little else. I was curled up on the chaise, my silk slippers discarded on the floor as I laughed at Charlotte's letter, when James entered and bowed.

"Lady Matlock, madam."

"Good morning, Elizabeth," said the same as she bustled into the room.

"Aunt Mary! What a surprise. I did not even know you were in town." We kissed, and she embraced me with great firmness.

"Well, we were not, but we are visiting Catherine and Anne. And when I heard you had been unwell, I insisted we stop here that I might see you." She stroked my cheek and held my gaze in a searching manner. I did not think Fitzwilliam would have confided any of the details of my ill health to his aunt, but maybe I did not yet have the measure of their closeness.

"Thank you. I have been unwell, but I am quite recovered now. It is very solicitous of you to call. I am touched. I hope you will stay to luncheon. Fitzwilliam will be very pleased to see you."

"He had better be. I imagine he will be surprised. I did not tell him I was coming, and he does not like surprises. Still, it would be no good for him to have matters exactly as he wishes the whole time, now would it?"

She winked, and I called for tea. Lord Matlock, I was told, was currently with his solicitor on a matter of business. After some conversation about Derbyshire and the Matlock's journey south, she leaned towards me and seemed to grow slightly grave. "My dear, I hope I do not speak out of place or too hastily. I can see you are looking very well, and I hope you are properly recovered… You are one of five sisters, are you not? And so your mother must have borne her children with ease. Maybe you are not aware that losing children early in your time is a trial known to many women. I lost two children before James was born and another between him and Richard. My sister Darcy also lost a child early in her marriage... Do I say too much?"

"No. No, you do not say too much." I looked away, shocked at how much she must have been told.

"And do not fear that this matter is widely known; it is not. I saw you were most particular about food at the Standenton Park ball. You avoided lamb, but you had eaten it without complaint when we visited Pemberley, so that gave me suspicion. I also thought you looked even more beautiful that night than you had before." She smiled sweetly and took my shaky hand in hers.

"When Richard reported that he had called here and been turned away by Darcy because you were grievously ill and kept to your bed, I feared things had not progressed as one would hope."

It was a relief to me to know her knowledge did not extend to my own rash behaviour, for I liked Aunt Mary very much and did not want her to disapprove of me. "You are quite the detective, Aunt Mary. Have you considered writing novels?"

"I have not the patience, my dear. In any case, Lord Matlock would never countenance my having anything in print! He would fancy me a revolutionary and live in fear of being defamed in some scurrilous story!"

We laughed, and I was surprised to be comforted by her presence. She had taken me lovingly and unnecessarily into her confidence. To feel her hand upon my knee and know she, too, had suffered as I had, was vastly moving. Before long, Fitzwilliam joined us, expressed great astonishment at his aunt's presence, and welcomed her warmly. To him, she said nothing of my state of health but said she was between stops on the way to Rosings and simply wished to see us. We dined on fish and sweet breads and talked of the Bellamys and the highwaymen who had never been apprehended.

"How pleasant this has been. You make me quite pleased I called. Tell me, do you have plans for this afternoon?" asked Aunt Mary brightly, turning a small spoon in her tea.

"Erm, yes. I am afraid we do." Fitzwilliam answered in a nervous manner. "We have made arrangements to call upon an acquaintance."

"'An acquaintance'? Come now, Fitzwilliam, there is no need to be coy, for you know nobody who is unknown to me, I'll be bound! Who is to have the joy of your company?"

I could see Fitzwilliam was searching for words, and so I precipitated him. "We are to call on Mrs Lovelace, Aunt Mary."

She looked at me and then at Fitzwilliam. She flushed and coloured. After a moment of silence, she recovered herself. "*Mrs* Lovelace? Surely not, Elizabeth. Fitzwilliam? I cannot approve of your subjecting your wife to such a person, and I am sure Lord Matlock would say likewise. Particularly as Elizabeth has recently been...unwell. It is too much; it really is. It was bad enough you were confronted by one of the daughters at Standenton Park. Lord Matlock and I agreed on the way home that evening that, had we known she would be there, we never would have attended. Good gracious, you will be bringing her to Pemberley next!"

"Now, Aunt, you know I would not. I know my responsibilities, thank you."

"In any case, Aunt Mary, it is I who wish to meet her...properly. I am sorry if it shocks you, but there it is. We would never dream of inflicting company on you that you did not deem appropriate. I cannot have you blaming Fitzwilliam for our familiarity in calling on her since it is all my own doing."

She exhaled, placed her saucer on the table, and looked about her. "Well, if you are resolved, then you are resolved. But you should know, Elizabeth, you do her a great and, I might say, unwarranted honour in recognising her. There are not many wives who would do so. What I say now, I say knowing I may shame your husband, but I shall say it in any case. I hope you do not think Fitzwilliam's family, by which I mean Lord Matlock, our sons, and I, would ever see *you* so disrespected."

"Aunt! I object—" Fitzwilliam's colour was rising, and his fingers were running through his hair in the agitated manner I had come to know well.

"It is all right, Fitzwilliam. Thank you, Aunt Mary. I appreciate your saying that, but I hope you know it is quite unnecessary. I am a most fortunate wife, you see. I know Mr Darcy is an honourable husband and... well...Mrs Lovelace and ladies like her hold no fear for me, so please do not be troubled on my behalf."

She looked at me enquiringly and, I believe, was satisfied. For my husband's dignity, I was glad the conversation had been brought to an end, for I do not believe he could have coped with any further discussion of our marriage before a third party, however much beloved. He was and is a very private man.

In the carriage on the way to Queen Anne's Gate, I felt a surge of violent energy. Mr Darcy, I knew, was uneasy, and I smiled at him from across the carriage, hoping his courage would rise as mine always did in me. I believe it did, and we passed a happy visit with Mrs Lovelace.

I had feared she may disobey Fitzwilliam and invite one or more of her daughters to join us, but she did not. We arrived to find her in much the same pose as I had found her upon my first visit. She was a small lady with a lined face, and her eyesight was better than her hearing. She told me she embroidered, read a little for diversion, and prayed her faculties would allow this to continue for as long as possible. Her ears, she regretted, did not allow her to enjoy music as she had in her youth. Her dog, it transpired, was also a friendly beast, and he and I became friends with little preamble. We three spoke of tea, novels, and Napoleon, and she was most solicitous of our comfort. After a fashion, even Fitzwilliam appeared at ease. She made no reference, in her lively and kindly conversation, to my previous visit, and she asked not why we had passed the hot, humid summer in town rather than at Pemberley. Neither did she, or anyone else present, mention her relationship to my husband's family. An ignorant witness to our visit would simply have taken her for a friend.

"I understand, Mrs Darcy, that you have been introduced to my eldest daughter, Mrs Woodham. She is newly married and still very excited with it. I hope she did not importune you. Alice is a good-hearted and loving creature, but to a new acquaintance, she can be...well...rather enthusiastic."

"I found her very agreeable, Mrs Lovelace—she and her husband."

"Yes, Mr Woodham is a very good man and a most steadying influence."

"Do you have any other family?"

"Yes, I have two other daughters. Sophia is next to Alice. She is seventeen years old and a wonderful pianist and singer. We all love to listen to her. My youngest is Frances. She is twelve and a lovely, quiet girl. Sophia and Frances both live here with me although they are presently away at Ramsgate, enjoying the sea air. Do you have brothers and sisters, Mrs Darcy?"

"No brothers but four sisters." I was careful not to mention Georgiana. "So I know all about living in a household full of girls!"

She smiled at my smile, and I glanced at Fitzwilliam, who did not seem discomforted by the turn of our conversation. I amused myself with thoughts of how he would fare in a household full of women. When it was time for us to depart, we stood, said our goodbyes, and thanked her. As we turned to leave the room, she surprised me slightly with her candour. "Thank you very much for your visit, Mrs Darcy, Mr Darcy. I lead a very quiet life and have enjoyed your company greatly."

I nodded in return and knew she had thanked me for my willingness to meet with her, knowing who she was and who she had been. Exiting her home, I felt quite undone. My hands shook slightly, and I experienced that strange blend of hunger and dizziness that often accompanies significant events. I found the dignity of Mrs Lovelace quite disturbing, but I was glad I had visited her. In the carriage, Fitzwilliam sat beside me and pulled the blinds down.

Chapter Seventeen

Not many days later, Fitzwilliam asked me if I felt well enough to return to Pemberley, and I answered him with pleasure in the affirmative. He was sorry to have passed most of the summer in the stifling heat of town and assured me that Derbyshire was at its best before the autumn set in. Dr Tranter visited me for the last time and said, as I knew he would, that there was no reason I could not undertake the journey. Georgiana, I believe acting on Fitzwilliam's behest, dragged me to the modiste to be fitted for several new gowns, many of them very comely. Last visits were paid to us and by us, and trunks were packed and loaded. We were to set off immediately after church and break our journey for two days in Hertfordshire, staying with Mr Bingley at Netherfield. Fitzwilliam had offered to stay at Longbourn, hoping, I believe, to assure me he held nothing against my family. Seeing his sacrifice and considering it unnecessary, I suggested Netherfield would be more convenient and less cramped, particularly as we would have Georgiana in tow. He agreed, likely with relief, and 'twas settled. And so it was as we entered the entrance hall of Darcy House on a Sunday morning, ready to be gone.

"Mr Darcy, Mrs Darcy, Miss Darcy." Parker, our butler, nodded sagely in greeting.

"Thank you, Parker. Is everything ready for our departure?"

"Yes, sir. Everything is prepared. But... well, while you were at church, the house has had a visitor. Mrs Darcy's sister is in the drawing room, sir." Astonishment was writ large on our faces—mine in particular.

"My sister? But Jane is certainly in Hertfordshire for I heard from her only yesterday." I led the charge to the drawing room. Opening the door, my eyes rested with alarm on my sister Lydia, who had established herself on my favoured chaise and was eating a piece of cake, a cup of tea in hand.

"Lizzy!" The teacup clattered against saucer as she bounded towards me with her arms outstretched. "I began to think you would never return. What awfully long services you attend! Well, are you not surprised to see me, Sister?"

"Indeed I am, Lydia. I—"

"And Mr Darcy, good morning. How tall you are in close quarters! I had quite forgotten—"

"Lydia, this is Miss Darcy, my new sister. And Georgiana, this is my youngest sister, Miss Lydia Bennet." Curtseys were made and pleasantries exchanged while my mind swam with questions. I could not begin to account for Lydia's presence in our drawing room, alone and without warning.

"It is a pleasure to meet you, Miss Bennet. We have so enjoyed having the eldest Miss Bennet here." I could see Georgiana trying to keep up her confident bearing in the face of Lydia's great brashness, and I was proud of her effort.

"Yes, Jane will have been an excellent caregiver, although I am not sure that I would have been. How confusing for you to have so many Bennets drifting about...well...it shall not be for long! What do you think, Lizzy? I shall tell you, for you shall never guess. *I am to be married*!"

"Married? Are you? Lydia, would you like to come to my chamber so we can discuss this? Have you been staying with Aunt and Uncle Gardiner? I am surprised they did not send me a message, but maybe poor Aunt has been too busy with all of the children—"

"Oh no, Lizzy. I had not even thought of our aunt and uncle. But now you say it, Aunt Gardiner may be able to help me with wedding clothes, do you not think? She is such a sage with that sort of thing. I have been in London not two days, and I walked here from our lodgings, for I knew you would be just the sister to help!"

"*Our* lodgings...Lydia?" Desperate to remove her from Fitzwilliam and Georgiana, I said, "Let us discuss this above stairs."

"Yes, of course, Lizzy, if you wish, but I have not finished my tea. And in any case, surely you wish to know to whom I am to be wed? I know you must be quite undone with the mystery of it! Well, maybe it would have been more fun if I had simply waited and visited you when it was done.

How shocked you would have been to learn that *Mrs George Wickham* sat in your parlour!"

Mortification, astonishment, and distress overtook me at such speed that I hardly knew how to act. Any dilemma I was facing, however, was soon removed when Georgiana, quite against my expectations, shrieked and fell in a faint upon the floor. There then followed a period of significant confusion. I sank to the floor and held Georgiana's face between my hands. Lydia cried, "Oh Lord," and Fitzwilliam rang the bell for help, hardly looking at me as he studied his sister's face. Servants flooded the room, and it was decided that Georgiana, who had substantially recovered herself at this point, should withdraw to her chamber and receive a sweet cup of tea. Fitzwilliam's expression was most serious.

"Elizabeth, would you step into the music room with me for a moment, please?"

"Yes, of course," I said, following close behind him. "But then I really must go to Georgiana. Whatever can have caused her to faint in that way? I hope she is not ill."

He closed the door behind me, looking deeply troubled. "No, you must talk to Lydia and find out what the situation is with Wickham. I will deal with Georgiana. Will you do that?"

"Yes, of course...but...what are you keeping from me, Mr Darcy?"

"There isn't time, Elizabeth. I will tell you everything, but we need to find out where Wickham is and what his intentions are. Do you understand why we must be quick?"

"No, sir. But if you wish it, I will be."

"Thank you, Elizabeth. I promise to explain the matter regarding Georgiana later. We will not be able to depart until we have resolved this. We cannot leave with Lydia here and Georgiana unwell, so I will ask Parker to have the carriage unloaded. Will you come to me after you have spoken with Lydia?"

I nodded my assent; he kissed my forehead and then was gone. The scene had done nothing to calm Lydia's spirits. "Poor Miss Darcy! I am so relieved I do not have a fainting disposition. Imagine falling down like that in front of one's acquaintances. I do hope she shall recover. She looked awfully pale."

"I'm sure Georgiana will be fine. Now, perhaps, I can hear your news more fully. What is this about being promised to Mr Wickham? And what are you doing in London? I thought you were in Brighton, staying with Colonel and Mrs Forster?"

"Well, I was staying with them to be sure, but *Mr Wickham loves me, Lizzy*! He loves me with all his heart, and we are to be married. I have been *much* in his company in Brighton." She paused, tilting her head and eying me in a way that gave me no comfort. "We have been to dances and assemblies. It was quite blissful, but once I knew he was to be my husband, there was nothing to keep me in Brighton. Wickham was eager to get away as he has business in town, and so I accompanied him. We arrived in town late on Friday, and I would have visited you before but—"

"Lydia, slow down! Do Papa and Mama know anything about this?"

"I do not believe they know yet. Mrs Forster knows, but she is a great friend, and she would not betray me. She planned to tell the colonel that I had missed Longbourn so much I needed to return. Is that not the drollest thing you ever heard? I have written to Kitty, but the letter may not have arrived. And in any case, I trust her to keep my secrets. I thought it would be more fun not to include them. How shocked they shall be!"

"Yes, I think you are right. They will be shocked to the bone. Have you told anyone apart from Kitty?"

"Why, I have told you and Mr Darcy and Miss Darcy and Mrs Forster, and I have written to Kitty."

"And where have you been staying in town?"

"We have been in a dreadful inn called the White Hart. It is in a ghastly lane off Regent Street, and it took me forty minutes to walk here. I have said to Wickham that we cannot stay there another moment, and he agreed I should have a house. We should not be kept to dirty inn rooms like beggars, and so I thought you might know how I might find a house."

"Lydia. Do you not think that, if you and Mr Wickham are to marry, you should do so before gadding about the country or taking houses or anything else? What of his position in Colonel Forster's regiment?" It was a great effort to keep my tone calm.

"Well, he has left the regiment, Lizzy. There was no future there, and Wickham has plans! He cannot allow the grass to grow under his feet."

"I'm sure he cannot. Now, Lydia, tell me: have you had...do you have separate quarters at the White Hart?"

"Oh no, of course not. You are a married woman, are you not? I am surprised you even ask such a question!" With this, she snorted and laughed a raucous laugh. How ridiculous under the circumstances that it was *I* who felt embarrassed.

"Yes, indeed. Now, where is Wickham? Is he at the inn?"

"I expect so. He has hardly been out since we arrived. He has to attend to so many matters."

"Well, why not stay here and finish your cake and tea, and I will be back shortly? Is that agreeable?"

She nodded happily, and it was plain that, despite her circumstances, she had no notion to run away. She simply plumped down in her seat and opened her mouth to her sponge. I found Mr Darcy waiting outside the door for me, and together we hurried to his study.

"How is Georgiana?"

"She is fine, Elizabeth. I think she is feeling rather foolish, but she is fine. Now, what has Lydia to say?"

My heart sank as I thought of poor, stupid, thoughtless Lydia, sitting in the drawing room, eating cake, and imagining herself a married lady with a house in town. "Oh, Fitzwilliam, I hardly know where to start." I looked away from him, and hot tears pricked my eyes. "She tells me she and Mr Wickham ran away from Brighton together. That they intend to marry but are not married yet. That our parents know nothing of her plans. That Mr Wickham has left the regiment for good, and they have been staying together in an inn near Regent Street since Friday night! I asked if they had been quartered separately, and she actually *laughed*. He is still at the inn apparently. Oh, it is too shameful!"

I felt his strong arms gathering me up and his kisses on my eyes. "Hush, Elizabeth. There is no need to cry. All will be well, my dearest. Hush."

"But whatever must you think of us after all that has happened before? And I know you have your reasons for forgiving Mama over her behaviour —but this! Lydia does not even realise that she has done anything wrong! She has not a thought for the feelings of our parents or poor unmarried Kitty or anyone but herself. If Mr Bingley were a different man, he might even abandon Jane over a scandal of this magnitude. Lydia has proved that she has no morals at all! I can hardly face you, Fitzwilliam, when you know this of my sister!"

"Hush. What is true of your sister was almost true of mine, Elizabeth.

That is why she fainted at the mention of his name. I believe it was a great shock to her to hear it spoken again and so unexpectedly. You see, Georgiana and I have not spoken of him since last summer. At that time, Wickham sought Georgiana when she was away at the seaside. She was persuaded to believe herself in love with him and to consent to an elopement." His grip on my arm loosened, and I was all astonishment.

"An elopement? Georgiana?"

"Yes. I did not tell you before because…well, it did not seem necessary, and I did not want you to think less of her as a result of this business. But the fact is that she agreed, and it was all fixed to take place. The only reason it did not come about was that I arrived unexpectedly, and she confessed to me. She was then but fifteen, which must be her excuse."

"Lydia is only fifteen."

"Well, in that, he is quite consistent. In Georgiana's case, I am certain his object was her fortune. As for Lydia, well, time will have to tell. I only hope he has not taken advantage of her absence from the inn to flee. Now I must write express to your uncle and father, and I will go to this inn to find the cad. If we can achieve a marriage as soon as possible, then in part her reputation will be saved, and it will likely have no influence on the prospects of Catherine."

"Thank you. You always know what is to be done."

"It is my role to know what is to be done, Elizabeth, and I will not see you in distress. May I leave you now? Please look in on Georgiana, and then escort Lydia to your Uncle Gardiner's home. I would keep her here, but I think an uncle is probably more suitable than a brother is to be her guardian. And in any case, I hope you understand I cannot have her chattering on about Wickham in front of Georgiana."

"Yes, of course. I would not dream of it. She must go to Gracechurch Street, but I should stay with her. I cannot leave her to my poor aunt."

Mr Darcy was not happy about this, but eventually, we agreed that I would accompany Lydia to Cheapside and stay with her at least the first night. It was a challenge to persuade her not to return to the inn, but I pleaded with her that she could not return there unmarried. In the end, I believe she was swayed less by my arguments than by the prospects of a ride through town in Mr Darcy's barouche. Whatever the inducements, she relented, and after sitting in silence on the way, we arrived at Gracechurch

Street. My husband's express had gone ahead of us, so my aunt knew what was afoot. My uncle had already left the house to join Mr Darcy at the White Hart, and we ladies were left in ignorance of what transpired there.

Our time together passed in boredom, anxiety, and frustration. Lydia sat in the window seat and talked of "dear Wickham" and his grand plans for the future. She continued to eat prodigious quantities while I had no appetite. When told that our father had been sent for and our uncle and Mr Darcy were working to assure her marriage would take place quickly, she was quite at a loss to understand the fuss and wasted no time in saying so. "Well, I cannot imagine why you are all being so dreadfully serious. After all, Lizzy, you only married Mr Darcy because Mama and Mrs Long saw him kiss you."

"Lydia!"

"Well, everyone knows. It is no secret. And has it not worked out jolly for you? Mr Darcy is a dour sort, but he is awfully rich, and he looks after you, does he not? In any case, it got you away from home, and that is what we all need to do. Lord! Mama is always going on about the difficulty of marrying us off, but when I find myself a husband, nobody seems to have a good word to say about it.

"But you have not got yourself a husband yet, Lydia! The problem is... you eloped, and you have been living with Mr Wickham, unmarried! Can you not see that?"

"No, I do not see that! I think you are all being awfully daft about it. After all, it will not be easy for Kitty and Jane. How many eligible men happen upon us, Lizzy? Hardly any. Mr Bingley, who seemed so hopeful, is gone, and when will another of his like come along? There is no one of our existing acquaintances. The regiment coming to Meryton was the best thing that has happened in years, and I am the only one to act on it. I do not see as I should be censured for it now!"

It occurred to me that she had been away from home for so long, she did not know of Jane's engagement to Mr Bingley. I could have berated her on the anguish she must have caused our parents or the impact on poor Kitty of the inevitable gossip, but there was no point. Lydia's mind was set. Her Wickham was as eligible a beau as any girl ever had, and nobody would disabuse her of the notion. What is more, her words fetched back to me the mood of Longbourn—the longing for something to happen and the ache to break out—and I knew that, in amongst her nonsense, there was a kernel of truth. With my silence, we were at a truce: Lydia eating her cake and me at a book borrowed from my uncle's library. Thus, we were eventually joined by my uncle and Mr Darcy, who both looked wan in the evening light.

"My dear Lizzy. Lydia!" snapped my uncle as he placed his hat upon the table. Our heads popped up like sunflowers, and my stomach turned with fear of what may or may not have come to pass. "Well, Lydia, Mr Darcy and I have just left Mr Wickham. We have spent a great part of the day with him, and we have ventured to make a number of arrangements, which I believe are satisfactory. I expect your poor father to arrive at any time, but I cannot think he will object to any part of the agreement. Indeed, I cannot see there is any choice. You shall be married from this house in two days' time. We shall obtain a special licence tomorrow morning."

"Married by special licence—how grand! But two days' time is far too short, Uncle. Why I need time to purchase dresses and—"

"Lydia, I am not opening a discussion on this subject, and I doubt my brother Bennet shall either. You have caused scandal enough, and you must be married as soon as possible in whatever clothing can be found for you in the time available. Let that be an end to the matter."

At this dressing down, the colour rose in my sister's face, and her expression was wild with fury. "If Mama were here, she would defend me! Lizzy, shall you not help me in this? It is not fair!"

"No, Lydia, I think Uncle is right. It is much better that the thing be done quickly."

Lydia glared at me, jerked up her arms, let out a teary shriek, and ran from the room. I was struck by how much she was still a child, and I was overcome with pity for her situation. If I had been unprepared for the married state at twenty, then Lydia at fifteen was far less so. All she knew of men were redcoats, dances, and flirting over card tables. She knew nothing of the strange intimacies of sharing a life with a man day after day: of making space for him alongside you, or of the elliptical mysteries of the flesh after its novelty had worn off. Her caprices would not always carry the day. She would have to contend with Wickham's vices and inadequacies, and her prospects were not good. She was a spoilt child of limited sense, and she appeared to have grand expectations of him. I wondered how she would fare, and I was most downcast.

With Lydia gone, it was explained that Wickham had not played the part of the willing bridegroom. He had a number of debts in Brighton, which motivated his decampment. Why he had taken Lydia with him was something of a mystery, but my uncle said they found no intention of his marrying her. He had only agreed to do so with the covenant that his debts were paid off and a sum of money paid to him to begin life anew. He was to take up a commission in Newcastle, which I thought had the merit of being far away. How this had been procured when he had effectively deserted from Brighton, I knew not. My heart ached to think of Fitzwilliam being forced into negotiations with the man who had tried to ruin his sister. I also thought it likely that my husband had laid out most of—or perhaps all— the sum required to bring this marriage about, and I was mortified. His penance for having looked down upon my family seemed to be long and arduous, and I felt great shame at their behaviour.

My husband reluctantly took his leave of me that night. He expressed concern should I become upset sharing a room with Lydia and suggested she would be well looked after by our aunt. I wished for nothing more than to sleep in his arms in our own home, but I could not in conscience leave my sister, so I stayed. She had had no supper and had spoken not one word to me when I joined her in bed. We lay together in the dark, shadows falling across the bed and unfamiliar noises of the eastern part of the city at night drifting through the windows. I knew Lydia lay awake, too. I felt with great sadness the sheer unluckiness of her situation. In my mind, I compared my nuptials to hers. By threat of scandal, I had to marry a stranger who turned out to be the best man I had ever known, and now I loved him as he loved me. Poor Lydia, I knew in my heart, would not be so fortunate.

"We shall see what we can do about a gown tomorrow, Lydia. I have some very pretty ones just arrived from the modiste that might do for you. You and I suit the same colours and are similar about the body, except you are the taller, of course. Hannah could let down the hems to fit you. We could change the ribbon or the lace to suit you. You may take my gown and make it your own just like we used to do at Longbourn."

My words seemed to settle on the bed linen between us, and I knew she was deciding whether to maintain her sulk. At length, she responded quietly, "Thank you, Lizzy. You had to wear one of Jane's did you not, so I suppose you and I are alike?"

"Yes, I did, and I suppose, in that regard, we are." I tried to sound light and hopeful. There followed a long and hollow silence before Lydia turned onto her front and looked at me.

"Oh, Lizzy, what will become of me?" And with that, her shoulders shook gently, and her tears fell. I took her into my arms and held her to me, whispering words of comfort.

THE NEXT DAY PASSED IN a tumult of activity. Fitzwilliam called at Gracechurch Street as soon as it was seemly to take me home. As promised, I came with Lydia, and together we selected one of my gowns to be altered for her. Hannah laid out all of the possible candidates on my bed in Darcy House, and I believe Lydia rather enjoyed selecting her favourite and then designing her amendments. She twirled about the room in a haze of pinks, blues, and greens and shrieked with joy as only my youngest sister can. Lydia's wedding gown was pinned, and Hannah stitched while my sister and I drank tea. "Is not this nice?" said Lydia with great optimism.

By late afternoon, it was decided that Fitzwilliam and I would accompany Lydia back to Gracechurch Street and then return home ourselves. When we arrived there, we found Papa had arrived and been appraised of the present circumstances. He sat in a chair in the corner of my uncle's study and looked grave. As he registered me, his expression softened slightly, and he stood.

"Elizabeth, Mr Darcy, Lydia." We each nodded. "Mr Darcy, I understand that I am to thank you for assisting my brother Gardiner in finding Mr Wickham and procuring the marriage that is to take place. Well, I do thank you, although of course, you are already familiar with hasty nuptials, so maybe you consider this quite unremarkable."

"Papa!" Anger and shame at my father surged in my breast, but I felt Fitzwilliam's hand on my arm and was silent.

"You are welcome, Mr Bennet. As for my thoughts on the present situation, I would be willing to discuss them but not in front of the ladies. I shall not have my wife distressed, sir."

I saw a shadow of defeat cross my father's face and knew there would be no more discussion of the subject. He glowered at Lydia and said, "Well... well. If you, young lady, had the same regard for the feelings of your poor parents and relations, we should not be where we are now. I would speak with you in private but later."

The taking of tea in present company was a stilted affair with Papa looking anguished and saying little. When Fitzwilliam suggested we return home, I gladly agreed. Inside the carriage, I pulled down the blinds and crawled into my husband's embrace. "How I have missed you, and it was only one night."

"Was your sister not a comfortable bedfellow, Elizabeth?"

"No indeed, she was most melancholy. When she is alone in the dark, I believe she sees things more clearly. Or more likely, when she is in the light, she feels compelled to pretend to an analysis of her circumstances that even she does not really believe."

"I do not know whether that is better or not. It is fortunate that she is not entirely without sense. But on the other hand, things being as they are, there may be an advantage for her to believe her own illusions."

"Fitzwilliam, I dread to imagine the trouble and mortification this business has caused you. I am sorry about Papa. I was astounded at his rudeness and so embarrassed. I must thank you on behalf of all my family for all you must have done for my poor sister. They, of course, do not realise how much you do by being involved, for they do not know what Mr Wickham is."

"Well, I think they know now, Elizabeth. For all he intended to do to Georgiana, he has done to Lydia, except I rather think he very much intended to marry Georgiana."

"Why ever did he take Lydia with him if he did not intend to marry her?"

"I think he was testing to see how far I would go to protect her. He knew the risk that I would force him to marry, and at the right price, he was willing. If I did nothing, then I suspect he would simply have abandoned her—suggest she visit the shops one afternoon and get away while she was out. He is calculating, but Wickham is also a man of impulse. As it was, he was not surprised to see Mr Gardiner and me in his doorway. I rather suspect he put the idea of Lydia's appealing to you in her head. What he was not expecting, though, and where I believe we had the advantage, was the involvement of Colonel Fitzwilliam."

"Your cousin? What did he have to do with it?"

"I sent him a message to meet me at the White Hart, and he was very useful. He could have arrested Wickham on the spot for desertion, and of course, he also has the right connections in the military to obtain this commission in Newcastle."

"How fortunate; although, I am embarrassed the colonel should be involved, but I am glad that he was helpful."

"He was, but of course, Elizabeth, it was gratifying to him, too. He is also Georgiana's guardian, and he has been waiting for his revenge on Wickham for too long. He was only too happy to assist."

"What shall we say to Georgiana?"

"Well, I think she should return to Pemberley straightaway with Mrs Annesley; we can follow later. As for this business with Wickham, well, should we not just tell her your sister is to marry Wickham tomorrow, they are to live far away, and leave it at that? What is your opinion?"

"I agree, but I think we should approach her together and assure her that Wickham will never come to Pemberley or Darcy House. She may occasionally be faced with Lydia, but rarely."

"Yes, Elizabeth, that sounds wise. Let us say that."

The marriage, which took place on the morrow, was an odd affair. After the bride and groom, only Papa, Aunt, Uncle, Mr Darcy, and I were present. We clustered at the front of the cavernous, city church like tea leaves. The vows were spoken to my uncle's rector, the register signed, and we were away. I took pity on my poor husband and did not insist we stay at my aunt and uncle's house for supper with the newlyweds. I took the view that he had been in company with Mr Wickham far more than was fair already. For myself, I was ashamed to think of the feelings I once had for my sister's husband. In the dusty light of the church, he seemed so diminished from the man I saw before my marriage. When he bowed low to me, held out his hand and said, "Sister," I saw in his eyes all of the obsequious deception and villainy that must have been there from the beginning. I could not regret our departure.

Hannah, having unpacked all of my belongings on the day we *should* have departed, packed them all again a se'nnight later. Given the choice, we would have departed for Pemberley directly after Lydia's wedding, but we knew the newlyweds wished to call at Longbourn on their way north, and we did not wish to be in company with them when we stopped in Hertfordshire. As it was, our extra days in town passed reasonably quickly. The heat of the summer had begun to wane. We dined with Colonel Fitzwilliam and his brother. I walked with my husband in Hyde Park, and we attended the theatre, where we kept largely to ourselves. We lay beside one another, hand in hand, living together like the strands of a knot.

Chapter Eighteen

The cool September air of Hertfordshire was a tonic indeed, and my heart sang to return to my childhood home in much happier circumstances than I had departed it. The soft hills on the edge of the fen country hummed with the activity of the harvest. The villages along the road passed us in a blur of familiar inns, cottages, and carts. Our carriage clattered into Meryton on market day, and all was as it should be, bustling and singing with the rhythms of ordinary life. It had been decided, after great cogitation, that we would stay our three nights in the neighbourhood at Longbourn rather than Netherfield. We did not have Georgiana with us, and with both Mary and Lydia married and from home, there was plenty of room, and the society of Miss Bingley and Mrs Hurst at Netherfield was not to be compared to Jane's at Longbourn. I believe Fitzwilliam was anxious I should be as happy as may be on this visit, and so he himself suggested this plan. He put on his most forbearing expression and assured me it was no sacrifice to him, and he would take cover in my father's library if the need arose. These preliminaries agreed, I had written to Mama, and three hours after leaving London, we rattled through the gates and down the dusty drive to Longbourn. What remained of my girlhood family gathered at the door to greet us. Mama flapped her handkerchief, Papa peered over his eyeglass, and Jane and Kitty, arm in arm stood behind with broad smiles.

Mama took me aside almost as soon as we arrived. "Lizzy," she whispered in a manner that was anything but quiet. "Will you come aside? I would have a private word with you."

"Coming, Mama," said I, handing my bonnet to Hill.

"Lizzy, you look very well, girl. I am pleased to see it. I must speak to you about sleeping arrangements for I must have Mr Darcy as comfortable as possible. Now, I can offer him the spare bedroom we keep for best, and you may have Mary's room if that is agreeable. Kitty was going to move into it, but she has not done so yet. Of course, if you think he would be better off in Jane's room, then I can evict her for the time you are here. It is a larger room after all and has a lovely view of the garden, but the bed in the spare is better. I thought I would leave it up to you since you know his tastes."

"The spare will be fine, Mama. I am sure Mr Darcy will be quite comfortable. But Mama, there is no need for me to separate. I do not want Hill and Sarah to waste time making up the bed in Mary's room. I can...well... I can sleep in with Mr Darcy."

She looked troubled—trapped between the titillating notion that my husband and I kept to one bed after nine months of marriage and the fear of offending him by not offering enough comfort. "I see, well, as long as you are sure, Lizzy. He will not think less of us, I hope, for not providing a suite of rooms for you."

"No, he will not, Mama. Please, do not trouble yourself about it. We will be very comfortable."

It occurred to me to say that, if Mr Darcy had a low opinion of her, it certainly was not by reason of her arrangements for guests, which were always generous and thoughtful. Her manner of obtaining husbands for her daughters, I knew to be quite another matter, but I forwent commenting on it. This detail being settled, we joined the others in the drawing room where I found, to my astonishment, Fitzwilliam conversing with Kitty. Her bobbing and blinking spoke of her nerves to be so singled out, and as I approached, I heard him suggest that she would enjoy visiting Bakewell when she stays with us in Derbyshire. She looked to me as a drowning woman may look to a life raft and extended a cup of tea in my direction with a wobbly hand.

"Ahh, Lizzy, Mr Darcy has invited me to Pemberley! I should love to come if it is no trouble to you. Shall there be balls?"

"Erm, well, there may be, Kitty, yes. We shall have to see. You will enjoy it even if there are none, I am sure. Mr Darcy's sister, Miss Darcy, is almost exactly your age."

At this moment, Papa announced his intention to retire to his library, and Mama suggested to Kitty that Mr Darcy and I be allowed our privacy to change and rest after our journey. Kitty, who had scarce finished her tea, pinned my elbow as we left the room and frantically asked in a whisper, "Is it true you have your *own* lady's maid, Lizzy?" I nodded discreetly and thought to myself that the education of my sister Kitty in the ways of dignified behaviour might be a long process.

When Fitzwilliam and I closed the door of the spare bedroom, we found Hannah within, hanging my gowns in the closet. "Thank you, Hannah, you are a wonder."

"You are welcome, madam. I assume you will wish to change out of your travelling dress, but do you think you will wish to change again for dinner?"

I thought, not for the first time, how Hannah was a girl of true manners and perceptiveness.

"Thank you, Hannah. As you have rightly guessed, we do not dress for dinner here. My day dress will be fine for the evening. I will dress for dinner tomorrow night when we dine at Netherfield and also the night after when guests are expected to dine here. When we are between ourselves, we are a little more informal, but thank you for thinking of it."

With this, she scurried out of the room with my green day dress draped over her arm, no doubt in search of a press. I went directly to my husband and threw my arms around his neck. "Sir, did I hear you invite Kitty to Pemberley and offer her day trips to Bakewell? Are you feeling quite well?"

"Well, I thought I may as well begin as I meant to go on. I must say, she seemed rather anxious about it. I thought she would enjoy Bakewell."

"I think she would if there were dancing to be had there! Thank you, Fitzwilliam; you are very kind, but you are allowed to be taciturn and aloof sometimes as well. After all, it is what people expect of you if you do not want them to become discomforted by your affability!"

I went to kiss him, and he met me with a friendly nip at which I laughed. "What did your mother want to speak to you about?"

"Our bedroom arrangements."

"Please tell me that is not true."

"Well," I said between kisses, "it *is* true, but I *am* teasing. She worried we ought to be offered two bedrooms and mithered over which two would be most appropriate. She is very anxious you should be comfortable, Mr Darcy, and she will not have you unsatisfactorily accommodated. Me, she does not care about at all. I told her one room would be quite enough. I hope I was not hasty?"

This question he did not dignify with an answer, and we passed a happy half hour, kissing on the counterpane. It was strange to think of my girlhood bed on the other side of the wall. Longbourn felt to me like an old friend who was no longer a best friend. I knew the ways of the house, and it had no surprises or discomforts. But it was no longer my home. My home was with Fitzwilliam, and I aspired to no other.

"I hope you will be all right at Longbourn, Fitzwilliam. I had forgotten how small this room is, and, well, if you find yourself excessively confined, tell me, and we shall walk out."

"You worry too much, Elizabeth. I shall be well. And your family are not as overbearing to me as you seem to think. After Lady Catherine's idea of hospitality, I can hardly play the critic, can I? In any case, Netherfield was the alternative. Had we stayed there, we would have had to contend with Caroline, and we both know what a trial she can be." He tightened his grip on my waist and kissed my neck. "I must admit that I have long considered the merits of bedding you at Netherfield, where I first desired you, against the merits of bedding you here, where you grew into a woman and lived as a maiden. And, well, although I would ideally like to do both, I prefer it here."

"Mr Darcy, you are a scandal. I hope you do not expect your conjugal rights these three nights, for how could I with my parents in such close quarters?" I teased as his kisses reached my bosom and beyond.

It was a couple of hours hence when we emerged, changed and little rested.

OUR SUPPER THAT EVENING WAS a quiet affair. Mama had been an assiduous researcher of my husband's favoured dishes and produced an excellent venison which we all loved. Excepting a couple of queries as to the size and number of various rooms at Pemberley, she surprised me with her restraint. She asked Mr Darcy about his sister and our neighbours in Derbyshire, saying my account of the Standenton Park ball had stirred her envy. She trained a sharp eye on him, seeing a man of great consequence whom she should not offend. She knew not his honourable and loving nature, but it occurred to me, as I considered him across the dining table, that only I knew the very best of him, and in many ways, that was as it should be. Jane and Kitty sat opposite each other. They were an odd couple to be the last of us at home, and no person of our acquaintance would ever have predicted Jane should remain a maiden after Lydia, Mary, and I were married.

Needless to say, plans for Jane's nuptials dominated much of the meal. For a wedding fixed for two months' hence, Mama had been hard at work, planning her trip to town, gathering cuttings, and pestering our aunt Gardiner about new warehouses. The wedding breakfast was a source of strain for the servants already; as for lace, ribbon, bonnets, and slipper roses, there was much to be said. Mama talked, Jane blushed, and Kitty's mind raced to keep up with the instructions Mama barked at her. Kitty was, I believe, broken-hearted to have missed Lydia's wedding. Had she known what a tawdry and empty affair it had been, she may have saved her tears. Her position as Jane's only bridesmaid, I hoped would console her. It did not escape my attention that Papa said little. He sat at the end of the table, turning his knife in his hand and looking solemn. He was not a man to be interested in wedding celebrations, and yet I knew there was more to his silence than Mama's prattling.

Later, we retired to the drawing room whilst Papa and Fitzwilliam retreated to the library. Later still, we all retired to bed. Fitzwilliam stayed downstairs reading while Hannah dressed me for bed. Barefoot, hair loose and in my nightgown, I padded next door to Jane to say goodnight, almost like old times.

"Come in," she said; I peeked around the door, finding her in the middle of our bed with a cup of hot milk.

The floorboards in various parts of the house creaked and moaned with the sound of my family about its collective ablutions. Through the walls, I heard Mama exclaiming to Hill on some domestic matter and Kitty dropping her water jug. "I came to say goodnight and sweet dreams." I closed the door and sat upon the bed with my sister.

"It is lovely to be here and to see you looking so happy. I should have hated to miss all of your wedding preparations, and as it is, Mama has done her best in a single supper to keep us abreast of developments!" We laughed as we always did when we were together.

"Yes, she has certainly done her best. I hope Mr Darcy was not too overwhelmed."

"Oh, I think it takes more than Mama to overwhelm Mr Darcy. I believe he is quite unscathed. I am more concerned about Papa. He was so grave and silent. He was not himself at all. He appeared even more severe than he had in London when he came to find Lydia. Tell me, how was the stay of Mr and Mrs Wickham?"

"Well, they stayed for four days, and the time passed peacefully. Mayhap at times, they were a little embarrassing, but that is all."

"Embarrassing? Lydia? Surely not!"

"Well, she was most particular to be treated as a married woman by us all, and with my engagement being known by the time they arrived, I am afraid to say she rather singled me out for marital advice. She gave me a most awful account of her private relations with Mr Wickham as I shudder to recall. She made it sound so dreadful that I can hardly even look at Mr Bingley."

"Poor Jane, I shall have to correct that. What about Mr Wickham?"

"Well, he was all agreeableness, to be sure. He was most attentive, making time even for Kitty and complimenting Mama on dinner. He was well behaved, but in company, he always was. I could not help but think he was not quite his old self. I saw him looking at Lydia as she talked and talked, and there was a sort of resignation in his eyes. I wonder whether he has been sobered by events. I believe we must hope that he really loves her."

"Yes, we must hope. But whether we can believe it, is another matter. Did he talk with Papa while he was here? I was shocked that Papa received them at all, I must admit."

"I do not believe he intended to, but Mama greatly desired it, and in the end, she prevailed. Papa and Mr Wickham spoke a little, but not at any great length as far as I know. Mr Wickham, as you know, has always been a man for the ladies. He is happy in the drawing room amidst the talk of fashions and assemblies where Papa is not. But there certainly appeared to be no ill feeling between them. I caught Papa chuckling on occasion when Mr Wickham made a joke. Apart from the embarrassment occasioned by their being here, there were no vexations attached to the visit."

"I am glad to hear it," said I, smiling and lying down on the folded counterpane beside my sister. "Now, I believe some practical marital advice is required." And so, we kept company long into my first night back at Longbourn. Jane's big blue eyes looked about, and she admitted to great foreboding. She confided that Mr Bingley had kissed her on the lips and stroked her ungloved hands on their walks. I told her she had had far more affection from him than I had from Mr Darcy before we married, and she must look upon this as a good sign. Mr Bingley, I was confident, had a warm and loving nature to match her own. I did my best to assure her with respect to her wedding night that she had nothing to fear. It was a challenge to do so without betraying too much of the passion of my nights with Mr Darcy. Indeed, I thought of the glorious power and soft, tender moments of his love, and I realised they were quite beyond description.

By the time I left Jane and returned to my chamber, I found Fitzwilliam abed and barely awake. "I thought you had deserted me, Elizabeth."

"Never, sir," I said as I crawled in beside him.

THE NEXT MORNING WE WERE joined by Mr Bingley who, having paid every civility to Jane, Mama, Kitty and me, went out for a ride with Fitzwilliam. After a polite period of chatter and embroidery with my mother and sisters, I excused myself and knocked on Papa's library door.

"Enter."

"Good morning, Papa. Do you welcome visitors at this hour?"

He put down his paper and adjusted his eyeglass. "Well, well. Yes, Lizzy. Come in." I thanked him and sat down on my favoured chair, expecting our conversation to flow as it always had. I was not to be satisfied for, after a period of awkward remarks on the season and enquiries as to one another's comfort, we were locked into silence. I selected a book of poems and sought to pass some time with it. Papa returned to his paper and then appeared to put it aside in favour of a novel. He did not tell me, as he might have done in the past, what he was reading. It seemed to me only candour would do.

"I hope I do not say too much, Papa, when I wish aloud that one day our old easiness with each other might be restored?" I looked at his face for a sign I might continue. None came, but I resolved that, since I had started, I might as well finish. "You see, I miss you greatly, and I am quite at a loss to account for your manner with me now. We have always been good friends, have we not?"

He took a great breath, put down his book without marking the page, and looked out of the window. Silence sat like a sow upon the floor between us. "We certainly were friends, Lizzy. You were my greatest friend in this house. If you think that I do not regret having lost you, then you are wrong.

Of course, I do. I regret it very much. I regret not having your company and your conversation. I regret very much that I was forced by threat of scandal to part with you to your husband. I believe his wealth leads him to a sense of great entitlement to all things, and maybe it led him to feel himself entitled to you. I do not know. But I know it fell far short of what I wished for you. You cannot expect me to rejoice in such a history. This business with Lydia...well, it has been a great blow as well. But, one might almost have expected it of her. One might almost have imagined her silliness and audacity could not be for nothing. From you and for you, I expected much better. I am sorry to say it, but there it is. You did suggest I speak the truth."

"Oh, Papa, is that what has been troubling you? Is that the cause of your silence—your strange, grave disposition since we arrived yesterday? Is that why you spoke not one word to Mr Darcy when he joined you in here last night? Yes, he told me of that. I asked him as I sought to establish your state of mind. He would not have said so otherwise, but I specifically asked about the conversation that passed between the two of you when you were left to yourselves. I worried so when he said you were silent. He is a man who can bear a silence better than most, but I know it is not your natural way." I placed the book of poems aside and leaned forward, beseeching him. "I am sorry the circumstances of my marriage gave you pain. At the time, they gave me pain too, and I was wretched when I left this house. I had told you the truth of what happened that night at Netherfield, and you had not believed me. I do not reproach you for it now although I might have then. In consequence, I found myself indissolubly attached to a stranger, a man of whom I had formed, if anything, a low opinion. I felt myself abandoned and entrapped. But Papa, I cannot have you believe I feel anything but the greatest contentment now. I love my husband, sir—love him very much. I know he loves me, and we are quite the happiest couple in the world. You cannot know how wonderful he is. The best part of him is known only to me, but it is there."

"Yes, yes, I know, of course. He has been remarkably generous in relation to Lydia's marriage. Indeed, I could never repay the money he laid out to bring it about. I do not fault his pecuniary generosity, Lizzy. That is not my point."

"It is not his generosity to Lydia of which I speak, Papa. Mr Darcy has shown his love to me and has cared for me more than I could ever have imagined. He has taken me into his confidence, protected me, and been attentive to my every comfort. Although he did not compromise me as Mama alleged, he did love me all the time, right from the start of our acquaintance."

He looked up, startled. The morning light poured through the library window in a pitiless manner. "I am sorry, Lizzy, but you will not persuade me. I thank you for trying as I assume it issues from some affection for me on your part. Your account of events at Netherfield is quite incredible, my dear, and you sport with my intelligence in delivering it as if it were a truth I could ever believe. As I have said, I do not fault your husband's willingness to spend his fortune, and I do not suggest he has no affection for you. But the sort of affection that leads a man to impose himself upon a gentleman's daughter in a public place and under the very noses of her parents is not the sort of affection I wanted for you." He stopped and, without waiting for me to speak further, picked up his book and fixed his eyes upon the pages. Exhausted and astonished, I left the room, straining not to cry.

I kept the details of this bitter confrontation with Papa to myself, and we were a happy party at Netherfield that evening, where Miss Bingley hosted a dinner in honour of Jane. Kitty joined Fitzwilliam and me in our carriage while Jane rode with our parents. Miss Bingley and Mrs Hurst were gracious and pleasant to us all. They were, I fancied, seeking at last to pay off every arrear of civility. How strange to think that, not a twelve month ago, I had been their unwelcome and unscheduled guest, tending to my ailing sister. It astonished me to recall how I had misunderstood Fitzwilliam's regard for me. His looks and subtle suggestions, which now I know so well, I had misinterpreted completely. For passion, I had seen censure, and for love, disapproval. It was not so now. When his eyes sought mine across the drawing room throng or when his hand brushed my arm as he assisted me into my seat at dinner, I understood him right well.

Chapter Nineteen

The very early morning found my husband and me walking out from Longbourn, bound for Oakham Mount, our breaths showing in the chilly air and our boots dampening with dew. It was a cold morning for September, but in my view, they were the best for a walk. We had decided upon this plan in bed the previous night, and since it necessitated getting up even earlier than Hannah, I had left a message for her with one of the maids that I had dressed myself to set out with Mr Darcy, and she could be at her leisure until I returned. As it was, we walked on even beyond the mount. I had visited the kitchens and purloined for our comfort some bread and milk. At the apex of the mount, I had had some of each before offering the same to Fitzwilliam. And although his expression spoke of surprise at such informality, he soon acquiesced. Thus fortified, we walked on down grassy hills, across open fields, along hedgerows, and under the cover of trees as they lost their leaves.

Therefore, we were exhausted when, at nearly luncheon, we returned to the house. At once, I apprehended a strange carriage stationed at the front door, and I was busy trying to make it out when Hannah dashed out of the kitchen door and started towards us. "Madam. Mr Darcy, sir. Lady Catherine and Miss Anne de Bourgh are here... Lady Catherine is in the drawing room with Mrs Bennet, Miss Bennet, and Miss Catherine Bennet. Mr Bennet has joined them this last half hour. Miss de Bourgh sits in the carriage although she has been invited in several times, I believe. They have been here for over an hour."

I could feel Fitzwilliam darken like a storm cloud beside me.

"Thank you, Hannah," I said. "We are coming. Hannah, do you have any idea why Lady Catherine is here? You may be as frank as you wish."

"Of course." Fitzwilliam agreed, entreating her.

"Well, madam, I was not present when her ladyship was admitted, but I understand from the housekeeper that she wishes to see Mr Darcy. She had travelled from Kent to Darcy House and found that you had gone away, and so she came here. Erm, I believe that she is rather put out at not finding Mr Darcy within, and . . . well, her raised voice has been heard from the kitchen."

It was agreed that Fitzwilliam and I should join the party in the drawing room at once. He was of the view that I should allow him to tackle her alone, but I was not willing in that scheme. It seemed to me, not only as his wife but also as a member of the family upon whom she had apparently forced herself, that I could not avoid the situation, whatever it was. Therefore, alarmed and inquisitive but united, we entered the room. There we found my family mute and agape while Lady Catherine held court.

"Darcy, where have you been? This is the second time you have kept me waiting this year, and I must say it is a new and disagreeable habit of yours. What can you have been doing out of doors all the morning? *These* ladies and *this* gentleman have been quite unable to explain your absence." With this, she turned a disdainful stare upon Papa, Mama and my sisters. Me, she failed to acknowledge. "I have been most uncomfortable and—"

"Aunt, if you do not mind, I believe that Mr and Mrs Bennet and their daughters have been importuned long enough. Would you care to take a turn with me in the garden?" He opened the door himself and tilted his head in a manner that suggested he would brook no opposition. None came, and Lady Catherine stood and made to follow her nephew. I stood, looking to him for a sign of what I should do. I found I did not quite know my role in the current drama, and although I was used to her treatment of me, I was shocked afresh that Lady Catherine had not even greeted me.

"Elizabeth, we have walked far this morning. Why do you not remain here with your family? I will return directly. Is that agreeable to you?"

"Yes, yes it is." He kissed my hand, seated me upon the chaise, and with his aunt in his wake, was gone.

After a period of shocked silence, it was established that the four ladies had been closeted in the drawing room for over an hour, and Papa had joined them when he heard shouting. During that time, Lady Catherine had spoken at length of her displeasure at finding Mr Darcy absent from Darcy House and her astonishment that he would condescend to stay in such a house as Longbourn. The proportions of the drawing room were criticised, as was its aspect. Lady Catherine also had no admiration for the hall, which she had found to be dark. She had spoken in detail about her connection to Mr Collins and his entitlement at my father's death to inherit the whole estate. I understood from Jane and Kitty's looks that Mama had hardly contained her tears at this being a subject of conversation. Lady Catherine's comments and complaints, it appeared, had filled all of the time she had spent with my family. They, aghast at the appearance and conduct of their unexpected guest, had said very little. I was given to believe that Papa had said nothing at the insults heaped upon his wife. Upon realising Anne sat in the carriage by the front door, several attempts had been made to fetch her, but her mother would hear nothing of it, apparently preferring the sickly girl be kept out in the cold. I went outside and entreated Anne through the window that she was most welcome to sit in the drawing room with us. She looked at me with the same eyes that had looked at the floor on that awful last evening at Rosings, thanked me, and declined. I left her to her isolation, struggling to imagine her true feelings.

For myself, I fell between anger, astonishment, and amusement. I do dearly love to laugh, and what reasonable person could not see the comic aspect of this? On the other hand, I knew Mama had been upset, and Fitzwilliam was mortified. For all that Mama was a silly woman and not above deception and conniving, I hated to see her so shaken in her own home by the rudeness of Lady Catherine. As for Fitzwilliam's feelings, I found that when he was unhappy, I was unhappy and concluded this was the nature of true love and affection. Before long, I could not help but pace the room, glancing through the windows as I went, scanning the garden for a sign of them. Finally, through the orchard they came, side by side and apparently at peace. Fitzwilliam towered over his aunt, his step as even as his expression was inscrutable. Lady Catherine's heavy skirts stirred slightly in the wind, and she occasioned a look up at her nephew. I could not read her expression. As they walked around the house, Kitty joined me at the window and we craned our necks to see the pair approach Lady Catherine's carriage. There Fitzwilliam handed her in and turned back into the house.

When he re-entered the drawing room, he made straight for Mama.

"Mrs Bennet, you must allow me to apologise for Lady Catherine's behaviour this morning. I am very sorry indeed that she has imposed herself upon you in this way. She is leaving now, and she sends her compliments. I trust that that is acceptable to you. I suspect you do not wish to bargain further words with her, but if I am wrong, do say so, and I shall fetch her here at once."

"No, Mr Darcy. Thank you, but no." With that, she looked at me as an actor not in possession of her script. Mr Darcy also turned to me.

"Elizabeth, Lady Catherine has something she would like to say to you if you are willing to hear it?"

"Yes, of course." I went to take his arm, but instead he gripped my hand and led me to the carriage where Lady Catherine sat waiting, her stern profile framed by the window, her daughter fidgeting beside her.

"Ah, Mrs Darcy. Yes, well, I am sorry not to have been able to speak with you properly. I . . . well, I hope you are well and you have a pleasant journey back . . . home . . . to Pemberley. Anne and I look forward to knowing you better in the future." She stopped, and her eyes closed briefly before she drew a great breath.

"Thank you, Lady Catherine."

"I am not quite finished, Mrs Darcy. I ought also to say I was mistaken in a matter about which I spoke to you on your visit to Rosings in the spring. I believe you cannot be in ignorance of my meaning. In any case, I was mistaken, and there is no need for you to concern yourself with it. Please, think of it as unsaid. Do we understand each other?"

"We certainly do."

"Good. Well, in that case, I take my leave of you, Mrs Darcy. Please congratulate your sister on her engagement on my behalf, and also send my compliments to your mother and thank her for her hospitality." Her eye quivered as she looked in my direction. Light fell upon her lined face, and she looked as though she were made of paper. I thanked her again, bid her and Anne farewell, and they were gone.

"Why ever did she come here, Fitzwilliam?"

"I am not sure even she could tell you that, Elizabeth. There is a kind of madness within her; there always has been, and I believe we have just seen it at work." He kissed my head and turned me into the garden. We sat on a bench in sight of the house among flowers past their bloom and talked. "She had got wind of our visit to Esther when Lord and Lady Matlock visited her. Aunt Mary would never have told her nor would my uncle. She did not say, but I assume she learned this from listening at doors or some other such behaviour. Her staff may have informed her of something heard by a servant, for I believe she has the whole damnable lot of them spying on her guests."

"Yes, I think you are right. She said as much to me."

"What did she say?"

"On that last evening at Rosings…before she said what she said about you, she told me she knew you kept to my bed as her servants told her."

"Great God! Is nothing private there? In any case, it sounds as though, by some means or another, a discussion between Lord and Lady Matlock about our visiting Esther was not private. It got to Catherine, and she came here to remonstrate with me. It goes without saying that I was not willing to discuss it with her. But I did speak to her of what she had said to you at Rosings. I told her you knew it was untrue, but I would not have such a thing go unremarked, and if she was ever to see me again, she would extend to you and your family the proper civilities, including an explicit retraction and apology."

"Well, it seemed to work. I do not know her heart was in it exactly, but she did your bidding. Thank you, Fitzwilliam."

As we returned the house, Papa appeared. I was most surprised, and a little hesitant to see his elderly frame hovering about the door. "Lizzy, Mr Darcy, would you join me in my library, please?" With that, he turned, and we hastened after him. When the library door clicked shut, he turned towards us. "Thank you, Mr Darcy, for the respect you have shown to Mrs Bennet and Lizzy today. I was impressed, sir, with the manner in which you dealt with your aunt, and I thank you for it. You appeared to show great care towards Lizzy. I…I saw how the two of you are with each other for the first time, and…well, I believe I have been under a misapprehension and must apologise for certain things I have said to Lizzy and certain things I have *not* said to you, Mr Darcy."

"Papa, I—"

"No, Lizzy. Allow me to continue now I am begun. Let me feel the weight of my responsibility. I am not afraid of being overcome by the sensation. You were right. I did not believe you about the *incident* at Netherfield. I considered what you said at the time, as I know what your mother can be. I considered it, but I decided it could not be the case. I decided she must be speaking the truth; otherwise, I could not account for Mr Darcy's behaviour. I could not account for his speedy—I may say *eager*—willingness to make you Mrs Darcy. He married you without a whimper, which made Mrs Bennet's account all the more credible. What is more, *he did not deny* having compromised you. That is how I reasoned matters. You did not seem to me to be a woman in love, but I believed your reputation was ruined. I feared that, if you did not marry Mr Darcy, then you would not marry at all, and...well, I did not consider I had any choice. If, as it appears, Mr Darcy's behaviour was based on affection if not strict obligation, then I suppose we have all been lucky, have we not? But I have been wrong not to recognise it before. It was quite wrong of me to dismiss your account of matters." I thanked my father for us both since Fitzwilliam looked almost too astonished to speak. I believe he was struggling to credit how previously my papa could have called me a liar.

The remainder of the day I spent in the company of Mama, Jane and Kitty, while Fitzwilliam kept close with Papa in the library. I confided to my family how I had been treated by Lady Catherine throughout our acquaintance and what she had said to me from her carriage. I could not mention her allegation that my husband kept a mistress nor the awful consequences of my having believed her, but it was a great weight off my mind to say to my own family how she had snubbed me. They were in little doubt that Mr Darcy must have spoken very harshly to his aunt, and it was, as far as they were concerned, no more than she deserved. It was agreed that poor Mary was to be greatly pitied for all the time she was obliged to spend in Lady Catherine's company.

That evening a party of some number was expected at Longbourn for dinner. All at Netherfield were invited as were Sir William and Lady Lucas and our aunt and uncle Philips. The imminent arrival of a large party of important dinner guests was, in my view, just the thing for Mama since it did not allow her mind to dwell on the disagreeableness of Lady Catherine's visit for longer than was healthy. Fitzwilliam readied himself quickly in order to leave the bedroom for me. As the light was lost from the sky outside, Hannah dressed me in a splendid grey silk gown that had been one of my London purchases. It had delicate lace sleeves, and it was cut low on the bodice with a fine pink silk band around the waist. I had deliberately kept Fitzwilliam from seeing it and thought it likely would become a favourite of his. It was Hannah's idea that I should wear the Darcy pearls in my hair rather than around my neck. "I believe that this will surprise the master!" she said with relish as she pinned them to my dark curls.

Hannah had dressed me to creditable effect many times, and I trusted her. She was, it transpired, quite right. As soon as I entered the drawing room for drinks, my husband treated me to one of his customary stares, his expression blank, and his eyes aflame. He had been speaking with Kitty, who chatted brightly on.

"What a lovely dress, Lizzy! Mama will be beside herself when she sees you in something so fine. And what do you have in your hair. It looks like a necklace. How very clever. I wish I had a maid to dress my hair every day!"

I thanked her and took my husband's arm into dinner. The evening passed in joy and gaiety, and I can hardly remember an occasion when I was in higher spirits. Jane looked serene and beautiful beside Mr Bingley, and his sisters continued their civil behaviour from the previous evening. In the glow of such a successful supper, Mama quite forgot the horrors of Lady Catherine's visit, and I even caught Papa casting her an affectionate glance. Mr Darcy forced himself to talk with everyone in the room, even Sir William, who commented loudly and with a wink on my comely appearance. After supper, the furniture in the drawing room was cleared to the walls, and we danced while Charlotte Lucas and I shared piano-playing duties. Fitzwilliam danced with every lady in the room, even Mama and our aunt Philips. I do not believe my family could credit what their eyes were seeing.

Chapter Twenty

We did attend Jane's wedding, which took place almost exactly one year after our own. By this time, I was again with child, and Fitzwilliam was white with worry the whole time we were away from Pemberley. It took all of my understanding and coaxing strategies, learned in twelve months of being Mrs Darcy, to persuade him to allow me to undertake such a journey. I did persuade him and was glad of it, for it was a joyful day. Jane was as serene and fine as I always imagined she would be on the day she was wed. My babe was showing very slightly, and I stroked its outline under my cloak as I stood in the church.

Kitty wore a beautiful gown and I believe was fussed over enough that her absence from Lydia's wedding was all forgot. In her finery, she caught the attention of a young cousin of Mr Bingley, who, some weeks after the wedding, returned to stay at Netherfield and began calling at Longbourn with notable frequency. Before long, he asked permission to court Kitty, and they were engaged and married in very little time. As I write this, they are happily settled in Bath and have two children to their credit. As an adult and a mother—and in isolation from Lydia—Kitty has grown so sensible you would hardly know her.

Lydia, after a great deal of fuss, attended Jane's nuptials on her own. It had initially been assumed that, with her being in Newcastle and out of funds, it would be impossible. Mr Wickham, of course, could not be spared from his regiment. However, Lydia performed histrionics by way of letters to Mama, Jane, and me until I relented and sent her the money for the journey. She settled herself in the front pew without shame and commented on people's outfits during prayers. For all of the trouble and mortification she has caused us, she is, in the final analysis and in the teeth of misfortune, resolutely herself and is to be given credit for it.

Mary and Mr Collins were also guests and appeared to be rubbing along as well as any two ridiculous people locked into holy matrimony might. A twelve-month later, Mary bore Mr Collins a lovely son, but they have not had further issue. Is it possible, I have wondered to myself, that my sister has denied her husband even his modest demands?

Lady Catherine, we did not see for over a twelve-month since, by the second Easter of our marriage, I was heavy with child, and it was not possible for me to travel. Fitzwilliam would not hear of my suggestion that, for the sake of family harmony, the Rosings party be invited to Pemberley.

"Certainly not, Elizabeth. What if the babe comes early? I will not have Lady Catherine here at a time like that. She is the last person you should be hosting in your condition. It is unthinkable."

As it was, we visited Rosings the following year with enough of our own servants that we did not need to trouble any in Lady Catherine's employ. Mr Darcy, it seemed, did not like to think the maid who changed his bed or the boy who polished his boots was reporting his every activity to his aunt. By the time of this visit, Colonel Fitzwilliam had married and attended with his wife, Cassandra, whom I like very much. We have persisted in the "Richard" and "Lizzy" business, and although my husband has never quite grown used to it, he does, I believe, benefit from a bit of teasing. As do we all.

With Lady Catherine, I have never quite achieved easy relations. I still find, this many years later, that she will fix me with a stare that would freeze a river, and if she can get away with cutting me off when I speak, she will. However, these complaints arise but rarely, and I find I can bear them perfectly well.

By contrast, her daughter, Anne, has emerged as a quiet friend to me. It happened on an overcast day in the second week of our second Easter at Rosings, and I was practicing the pianoforte alone when the door squeaked open. "Good morning, Cousin Elizabeth," said Anne as she walked into the room, touching her handkerchief to her nose and smiling. I knew then that her very address to me was a peace offering. "Would you mind if I joined you? I have some embroidery I would like to work on, and some musical accompaniment would suit me right well."

"Yes, of course. Miss de— or should I call *you* 'Cousin,' also?"

"I would like it if you would."

"Thank you."

After that, it became our practise, while Lady Catherine was with Mr Collins in the morning, that Anne would bring her embroidery to the music room where I would play, sometimes upon her request and sometimes, more testily, in rehearsal for the evening. I never knew her to contradict her mother directly, and she did not become outgoing in her behaviour. She had been silent too long to ever really change. But we did reach a friendly and quietly convivial understanding, and I was glad.

When we have not been visiting relations, we have lived a settled and happy life here at Pemberley. I have continued on my tenant visits and seen many more families multiply on the estate. Fortunately for Mrs Ashby, she has had no more children, and her husband is now fully recovered from his illness.

Hannah is still my lady's maid and, this spring, turned down a marriage proposal from a local tenant farmer. It was a shock to all who knew her that she would do such a thing. He is a respectable man, and she is a woman not getting any younger and in domestic service. I found myself lobbied by Mrs Reynolds, by Hannah's married sister, who wrote to me, and even by Fitzwilliam to intercede on the man's behalf. For myself, I could see their point. As much as I would have missed her if she had married, how could she deny herself an establishment of her own with children and the potential for love? These were the arguments as I presented them to Hannah. Yet, she remained unmoved. She continued to brush out my hair and, straightening herself, fixed my eye in the mirror of my dressing table.

"I know it is hard for others to understand, Mrs Darcy, but I am quite sure it is the right thing. I see what love looks like, and I know I do not love him, and he does not really love me either. People may think me a fool, but there it is."

"You know love can grow, Hannah. It can grow, sometimes from nothing, over time, but you have to give it time."

"I know it can grow, madam, but... well, if I may be so bold, I do not think it will grow from nothing. I think the seed needs to be there. I am sure there is no seed between us, and if I say no, he will surely find another woman who can make him happy."

I chewed over her words. "Maybe he will, maybe he won't. I do not know, Hannah. None of us can know the future. If you are resolved, then you are resolved, but I hope that you are not taking this step because you do not want to leave Pemberley. We are such good friends, you and I. If you were to leave, I am sure I would not find an equal to replace you, but that must not stop your grasping happiness if it is available. You know, if you were to marry, that you would still come here, you could visit... we would still be friends."

"That is a very kind thing to say, Mrs Darcy. Thank you." And with her simple, direct words, the matter was closed. I recalled my own reaction when Mama had ordered me in the garden at Longbourn to marry Mr Collins, and I could not find it in me to censure Hannah's decision.

Our sister Georgiana has gone from strength to strength. When, in the tail end of that humid summer in town, Fitzwilliam and I told her that Wickham was to marry my sister Lydia, she took the news better than either of us had anticipated. She nodded, exhaled, looked slightly anxious, and said, "Thank you for telling me. Is your sister well, Lizzy? I do hope she is and she, they... I wish them much joy."

Later, when Fitzwilliam was closeted in his library, she approached me alone and owned to being embarrassed for having ever loved Mr Wickham. I took her sweet face in my palms and entreated her. "Oh, Georgiana! When we are young and foolish, we are young and foolish. We all are, and you were no worse than others have been. We have all thought the wrong thing and been mistaken in our acquaintances. It speaks well of you that you trusted him and saw the best that may have been in him. You must not reproach yourself now. He is married and far away, and you have everything before you."

She did, as it turned out. For within the twelve-month, Georgiana had been presented at court, and within the eighteen-month, she was married to her first suitor, Lord Avery, whose estate was not fifty miles from Pemberley. When the time for Georgiana's presentation drew near, I realised there was a matter, long dormant, that had to be addressed. I found Fitzwilliam in his study about his papers and sat in the chair opposite him.

"I know that look, Elizabeth. Am I to have a scolding?" He smiled, teasing me with my own words.

"Of course not, Fitzwilliam; for you, *as you know*, have done nothing wrong. No, I was just thinking of Georgiana's coming out and how close it is getting. We only have two more weeks in Derbyshire, and then we shall be off to town. And then only a week to prepare before presenting her and hosting our own ball. There will be so much to do. Mrs Reynolds tells me that Lady Broughton's housekeeper told her that *five hundred* sandwiches were eaten at Diana Broughton's coming out..."

He leaned back in his chair, his lips turned up at the corners, and his eyes on me. "I am sure that is true, Elizabeth, but you have not come here to talk about sandwiches surely—particularly, other people's sandwiches?"

"No, but I do mean it when I say we shall have so much to do when we get to town. We shall be so busy getting things ready, and there will be little time for conversation...for being together like this—"

"Out with it, Elizabeth! What is this great matter that requires discussion?"

"Well, it is Georgiana. She has gained so in confidence and is obviously going to sparkle in London. She will be exposed to society in a way she never has been before. She will meet people, and she will not have us standing over her. She will meet people, and they will talk... Fitzwilliam, you know what the world is, what gossips people are. If you do not tell her about the Lovelaces, then somebody else will. If you tell her now, she will have a little time to digest it, and you can give her your truth about them. She is eighteen years old, and...well, she may be a married lady inside the year."

He turned away at this, slightly discomforted by the thought. I had prepared myself with argument upon argument and anticipated what he might say against me. I had imagined raised voices and my having to beg him to be sensible or even threaten to involve Colonel Fitzwilliam. But in the event, it was quite different. After a pause, he turned his body to mine, took my hand, and said, "Yes, Elizabeth. You are quite right, of course. Shall we seek her out now?"

When we found Georgiana with her book in the drawing room, I quietly dismissed Mrs Annesley and let Fitzwilliam do the talking. She was, I believe, very surprised, but she was not angry or resentful either at the history or at having been kept so long in ignorance of it. Her eyes widened a bit when she learned of her three sisters, but she did not seem unduly scandalised, and later, after supper, Georgiana suggested she meet them when we were all in town.

So it was that Alice Woodham had her heart's desire. After some discussion between Fitzwilliam and me and correspondence with Mrs Lovelace, it was decided that Georgiana's first engagement upon our arrival in town would be a visit to Queen Anne's Gate. Mrs Lovelace, Miss Sophia Lovelace, Miss Frances Lovelace, Mrs Woodham, Georgiana, and myself sat about Mrs Lovelace's parlour and smiled over teacups while Mr Darcy, Mr Woodham and Colonel Fitzwilliam, whom Georgiana specifically requested be present, stood, looking only a little awkward. Mrs Lovelace's little dog wagged his tail against the hearth. Nothing was spoken of the relations between those present, but everybody knew. It was a kindness to the girls that they be allowed to meet their sister thus, and it was a kindness to Georgiana that she should be in ignorance no longer. I understand that Georgiana, as Lady Avery, has kept up correspondence with both of her adult sisters and discreetly visits with Mrs Woodham when in Derbyshire, as do Fitzwilliam and I.

Our own visits to town have been limited, to our great delight, by the arrival of our two daughters: Anne, who was born in the second summer of our marriage, and Emma, in the fourth. I know Fitzwilliam would like a son, and with four sisters by birth and four by marriage, I am scarce less eager for one myself. As I write this, my belly swells beneath my hand, and so we have every reason to hope.

Author's
Question & Answer

Q Since the story is told from Elizabeth's point of view, I think it would have been interesting to be witness to what Mr Darcy confesses to Mr Bennet at the Netherfield ball. If you were to write a short scene, how might that have gone?

A It is a downside of telling the story from one person's point of view, that there are a lot of "holes" in the narrative. Important things happen, but Elizabeth is not there to witness them. Imagining what might have happened in those "holes" is part of the fun of reading and what a lot of fan fiction is about. In this story, the discussion between Mr Darcy and Mr Bennet at Netherfield is one of the most tantalising. My vision goes something like this: Mr Bennet, as we all know, is not one of life's dancers neither is he a social butterfly. I imagine him standing at the side, maybe telling himself a joke. He hardly knows Mr Darcy and all that he has heard of him is negative. As Darcy approaches, Elizabeth's father probably thinks that he is after speaking with somebody else. He would be astounded that Darcy is singling him out. As for Darcy himself, we must assume his head to be crowded with emotion. Firstly, his mind is reeling with his good fortune. He can see how things will be, and it is to his liking. In counterpoint to that, he is embarrassed. He is not a man who likes his private life to be public property. He will be ashamed of the need to tell a gentleman that he has been observed compromising his daughter. Is Darcy troubled by Elizabeth's apparent lack of affection for him? I do not believe he is. He sees she is not in love, but he assumes his love will be powerful enough to carry her along and, in time, she will love him. In this moment, he feels lucky. The dice have fallen exactly right, and he is too arrogant to lose time worrying about how Elizabeth sees things. Darcy is a man of action and an audacious character. If something needs to be done, he just does it. Will he fudge it? Will he say it straight? For privacy, I think he would ask Mr Bennet into a side room, and then he would say simply that Mrs Bennet has observed him alone in a room with Elizabeth in a compromising situation and he is willing to marry her as a result, but to prevent further scandal, it may be best if the whole family removed from the ball. His pride, in my view, would prevent his making an apology. His kindness, in my view, would prevent his casting doubts on Mrs Bennet's veracity. What about Mr Bennet? I imagine him being speechless for a moment and no doubt very offended. However, for all that, he is a negligent parent during "normal time"; in a crisis, he does know what needs to be done. Mr Darcy is, as we all know, a very commanding character. And so, I do not envisage much argument or even discussion between the two men. In the moment, Mr Bennet will do as Mr Darcy says, and his resentment will be left to develop at leisure.

Q Elizabeth names her horse "Mrs Wollstonecraft." What was the significance, and why did she think Darcy enjoyed that?

A Mary Wollstonecraft was a feminist writer, educationalist and philosopher of the late eighteenth century. She was famous in her lifetime for promoting the education of girls and for her belief that women were not the intellectual inferiors of men. She had a number of unconventional relationships in her life. One way or another, her name was a byword for provocation and scandal. Why did Elizabeth choose this name for the horse that Darcy gives her? Well, I do not see Elizabeth as a dyed in the wool proto-feminist or a revolutionary. But she is well read, contrary, and intellectually bold. In the original, she verbally jousts with Darcy every time she sees him. However, in this story, her ability to directly challenge him is effectively stymied by her early marriage. She would enjoy more freedom than she has. I imagine her giving her horse a provocative name as a minor rebellion against this. However, far from annoying Darcy, he immediately sees the humour. It is redolent of Elizabeth's spirit, and so he enjoys it. And of course, in this story, Darcy is far less of a stranger to scandal than Elizabeth thinks he is, so maybe he is laughing at that as well.

Q I liked that you made Mrs Forster part of the scheme to get the couple away from Brighton with a simple fib to her husband, so Colonel Forster could not write the Bennets. Therefore, do you believe it was Wickham's intent all along to get money from Darcy, or was she just a bit of muslin?

A My reading of Wickham's motives in Jane Austen's *Pride and Prejudice* is that it is most likely (although by no means certain) that Lydia was just a bit of muslin whom he would ultimately have abandoned. Any variation story in which Elizabeth marries Darcy before Lydia runs away with Wickham drives a coach and horses through this because Wickham knows that Darcy will spend money to protect his wife from scandal. So, as to Wickham, I definitely think that he was trying his luck with Darcy's generosity. His instinct was that Darcy would be willing to do what it took to protect Lydia's reputation. My vision is that Wickham deliberately encouraged Lydia to visit her married sister in order to kick start the chain of events that then followed. I imagine Lydia suggesting the conspiracy with Mrs Forster to Wickham and him realising its possibilities. After all, he had already been foiled in his attempted elopement with Georgiana. He would have had no intention of being beaten again. If Mrs Forster could be held off writing to the Bennets, then that gave him extra time to make sure that there could be no doubt about their relations and to enable Lydia to drop the bombshell on her married sister herself.

Q I enjoyed that Mary Bennet marries Mr Collins, securing Longbourn for her family but also making herself a good match—on so many levels. Most *Pride & Prejudice* alternatives follow canon and have Charlotte Lucas marry their odious cousin. What inspired you to make this welcome change?

A I have always thought that Mary would have been an ideal choice for Mr Collins. The problem in the original (if you can call any part of the original a "problem") is that prior to his proposal to Elizabeth, Mr Collins does not notice Mary in comparison to her more obviously attractive older sisters. Then after his proposal has been rejected, his pride will not allow him to consider trying another one of the Bennet girls. Charlotte Lucas falls into his lap and offers him an ideal way out of an embarrassing predicament. However if Elizabeth had never rejected him, if his pride had never been injured, he would have had neither the incentive nor the imagination to look beyond Longbourn.

Q Why do you think Mr Darcy Sr never married Mrs Lovelace even after Mrs Darcy died?

A In my mind, he would have wanted very much to marry Esther when his wife died. However, he would ultimately have been held back by propriety and the perceived need to protect his legitimate children from scandal. The division between the two sets of siblings is a cause of tension in this story, and it would have been even more so in the aftermath of the death of Lady Anne Darcy when Georgiana was very young and the whole matter more raw.

Q Do you think that maybe Darcy suspects she might be with child as she is sleeping more during her first trimester and, of course, the eventual slight baby bump?

A Although it may seem obvious to us, I do not think of Darcy as having any idea that Elizabeth is pregnant. When it comes to her being sleepy and feeling a bit poorly, he would not have had enough awareness to understand the significance of these things. I am sure that other members of the household, in particular the ladies, would have guessed immediately. Women generally have (in my experience) a much stronger instinct for these things. Darcy is a man who had had very little contact with gestating women in his life. Would he have noticed changes in her body? He is very interested in her body, and he may have seen slight alterations, but again, I do not see a line between that and him guessing that she is carrying a child. At four months, some women are barely noticeable, and I imagine Elizabeth falling into this camp. In addition to this, my idea of Darcy in this story is that he is so obsessed with Elizabeth that he fails to think things through. He does not think enough about what she may or may not be going through. His mind is, in some ways, too focussed on his love for her and not enough on the lady herself.

Acknowledgements

To MICHELE AND ALL AT Meryton Press for including me. I am still surprised and very honoured, so thank you. Christina, you have made this book immeasurably better and been a great source of humour and ideas. I may never write "that" with a clear conscience again. Ellen, thank you for your keen eyes and amazing knowledge; Sue's "Regency Encyclopaedia" sounds like a website I need to visit. Zuki, thank you for producing a lovely cover with a real feeling for the story.

THANK YOU AND "I LOVE YOU" to my husband, and thank you also to my mum.

To THE STAFF IN MY local coffee shop in London, who kept me supplied with lattes while I held my nursing son with one hand and typed my first novel with the other, I thank you too.

To ANYONE WHO READS THIS book, thank you for taking the time and I hope you enjoy it. I am now on twitter so please do follow me @JenettaJames or find me on facebook at https://www.facebook.com/jenettajameswriter.

CPSIA information can be obtained at www.ICGtesting.com
Printed in the USA
BVOW08s0406091015

421359BV00002B/74/P